Dedication

For Andrew,
Your continued love and support amazes me every day,
I have found my mate and I've never been happier.
All my Love,
A.

Chapter One

*B*ang.
Bang.
Bang.

Cameron jolted awake and glanced at the clock. Just past seven. *Fuck.* He groaned and rolled over. The banging continued, and he prepared to get himself to crawl out of bed at the godforsaken hour. Then his brain clicked in—the knocking came from within his mind. He pulled a pillow over his eyes. "*Go away,*" he grumbled at the intruder.

"*Oh, good. You're awake,*" Jaden replied, well her mind-speak anyway.

In the two-and-a-half years they'd been partnered together, he'd never heard her say a word. At the moment, he didn't know if he could cope with auditory as well as mental harassment this early in the morning. "*No. I'm not. Go away. Can't you use a phone like everyone else?*"

"*Have you known me to ever use a phone? I don't even think I own one.*"

"*You have a department-issue cell phone. I think it's in your glove box. Why the knocking?*"

"*Really? I didn't know that. It's probably dead anyway, and I was knocking because I couldn't reach you. You were asleep.*" She let out a mental huff, as though she was annoyed at the idea he'd been asleep.

"Some of us need sleep, Jaden." Not that he would be getting any more. The last time he had a full night's sleep was when he took off to his cabin, two-and-a-half hours outside the city, and more or less out of his partner's range.

"We need to catch a kidnapper and a killer," she retorted. *"I'll be there in twenty."*

"Make it forty. I need to get ready." He threw the covers off and sat up, letting his exhaustion flow through to her.

She sighed. *"Fine. You get an hour, but if you're not down here waiting, I swear to God...."* She left her threat hanging—as she often did—then shut him out.

He tested to make sure she'd left him alone before he wandered into the bathroom, where he messed around for a while before starting the shower. The near-scalding hot water beat down on his back.

It already felt like one of those days he needed someone to remind him why he liked his job. Jumping from being a junior homicide detective to an elite investigator in Toronto, the largest city in Canada, he had more respect and power than most police commissioners. He should be grateful to be partnered with one of the most powerful known telepaths, but damn, some days she drove him insane. Concealing her talents from the public had been a minor miracle for years. One of his main jobs was to keep it that way. Most commonplace telepaths generated their own reality TV shows. Jaden? She possessed more power than all of them combined.

"You're still in the shower. Move it!" Her impatient voice popped into his head. *"You're running late."*

"Go away, Jaden." He hated having her barge into his thoughts at random times, along with a million of her other demands. In general, she gave him his privacy, only intruding when they were in close proximity or when she needed to contact him. Whatever the new information she'd discovered on this case it had gotten her all riled up.

She huffed as she left again. This time, he created a mental block, not caring she might get mad at him for the rest of the morning if she noticed. She always got pissed off when he exercised the tiny bit of control he had over her.

Fortifying his block, he went to work, soaping his body. He must be one of a handful of cops on force who didn't let the brilliant, but young, psychic read every single facet of his mind.

He finished in the shower then sauntered into the bedroom to get dressed. The clock told him he still had twenty minutes before Jaden would be there.

He towel-dried his hair as he pulled a suit out of the closet. Dressed, he grabbed a granola bar on his way out the door. He arrived at the front of his school-house-turned-condo building and took his mental block down with time to spare.

"*Here,*" Jaden announced, a second before her SUV appeared around the corner.

She slid into the loading zone in front of his building. He climbed into the passenger seat, and, the instant his door closed, she zipped into traffic, heading toward the station.

"*So, what's this knocking at an ungodly hour?*" He glanced at his partner as he buckled his seatbelt.

She tucked long jet-black bangs behind her ears and shot him an annoyed look. "*I was trying to get your attention.*"

"I got that, thanks. Why?"

"*I talked to a little girl last night.*" Jaden found a hole in traffic and barged through, ignoring the glares from other motorists. She always drove—he couldn't focus on her mind-speak and operate a vehicle at the same time. He cringed as she merged too close to a car behind her. Traditionally, the junior partner did all the driving anyway. He hated it most of the time.

"I thought you couldn't talk to the dead." He spoke aloud and then cursed himself for doing so.

She glanced at him, exasperated. "*For the millionth time, I can't talk to the dead. I'm not a medium. They don't even exist,*" she said, frustration creeping into her voice. "*I had a break through. She was able to share a lot with me.*"

"*Marissa is alive, then?*" Hope soared. They'd been on the case for four days with no luck discovering any leads in the girl's disappearance. Her first time walking the three blocks home from school, and she'd disappeared. The only clues—a tall dark man and, of her own free will, her getting into a non-descript beige sedan. With no hint to her whereabouts, they worked on the probability she was already dead.

"I didn't say that. I said I talked to a little girl. One from the missing files."

He bit back a sarcastic response. Right, a little girl from the missing persons' files. Ruth, their unit's administrative assistant, had pulled all missing persons' cases for the past ten years involving little girls in the same age range as Marissa, in the off chance this was a pattern. There were well over a hundred matches. That's where Jaden came in. If she could get a good sense of a living person, she could find anyone and try to communicate with them. An interesting science, but not exact. She needed details—a photo, a name, a birthday, a dwelling—something to hone in on.

"So, I think Marissa might still be alive," she finished. Crap, he'd zoned out on her.

"Repeat that." He hated when he raised his block too high and missed what she said. He found the balance difficult sometimes, to keep his thoughts to himself but still communicate with her.

"Cam," she said, with a mental sigh, *"she's been missing for over six months, but she's still alive."*

"Wait who? Marissa has only been missing for four days."

"Jesus do you ever listen to me? Emily Knight,"

"Right."

"She's being held captive by a man. She thinks a new girl who joined her looks like Marissa. So there's a chance she might be alive. The girl also said there were others, but they've all gone."

"Why can't you talk to Marissa?"

Jaden clicked her teeth, one of the few ways she communicated out loud with him. Most often, it expressed her annoyance at his speaking aloud, although she never gave him a straight answer as to why she preferred to communicate with him mentally rather than verbally. "*You try being a disembodied voice talking to a terrified nine-year-old. Let alone getting her to answer.*"

"*Then how did you reach this other girl? What's her name?*"

"*Emily Knight.*" She sent him a mental snapshot of her photograph.

He could see the school photo of a girl with a gapped-tooth smile, blonde hair pinned in pigtails, and a clean and pressed school uniform. She could be Marissa's sister. The next image wasn't as nice. She had a dead look in her eyes, one he had seen all too often in the victims he'd dealt with. Her hair appeared knotted, her clothes covered in dirt, a smudge of something that looked suspiciously like blood on her cheek. She seemed to be in a basement or cellar of some sort.

She snapped the image away as he shivered. "*Jesus. I hate when you do that.*"

"*Sorry, I should have warned you.*" She reached over and squeezed his knee. "*I know you hate seeing things like that.*"

His pulse quickened. Despite their platonic relationship, Jaden affected him. Every time they touched, he realized how much he wanted her. He always shoved it aside—well, most of the time. They had a job to do. "*How did you reach her?*"

"*I used the Dreamworld. Implanted myself in Emily's dreams. Then I became an imaginary friend in her waking world. It's taken a couple of days, but I got through to her this morning when she gave me those images.*"

"*It's a bit manipulative.*" He knew finding people, talking to them, was what Jaden did best. He still had a ton of problems with the legality of it.

More teeth clicking, this time followed by a sharp turn, which brought them into the parking lot of the local coffee joint a few blocks from their office at police headquarters. "*Again, try explaining to a nine-year-old that you're a telepathic cop trying to find her and her captor. Trust me, it's better this way.*"

"*I just don't want you to do anything that might be*

considered questionable. The new laws coming into place mean telepaths might be compelled to take the stand and testify when they use their alibies. How is it going to appear when the defense asks you how you established communication with Emily? And you say 'Oh, you know, I pretended to be her imaginary friend to gain her trust, so she would tell me where she was being kept and who was keeping her.' It might be too hard for a jury to buy."

She shrugged and climbed out of the SUV. *"Not like there are many of us out there. The ones that do exist aren't as powerful as me. Besides, I'd like to see them try to put me on the stand. How can they record my testimony if I don't say anything? Coffee?"*

Dammit, he couldn't argue with the point.

She slammed the SUV's door. The hint for him to go order them coffee so they could discuss the case away from the broom closet that was the Special Investigations Unit. Jaden avoided using her mental abilities in public places unless she had to. If she did, she would mouth her words so whoever she was dealing with didn't get spooked. Realizing they could hear her when she didn't speak aloud shocked most people.

He followed her into the coffee shop. She pulled out her laptop. *"What do you want?"*

"Black tea and one of those cream cheese muffin things. The pumpkin kind."

He nodded and got in line. The lady in front of him counted out the cost of an extra-large coffee and a cookie in nickels. He tapped his foot as he waited. At least a cute guy wearing a tight pair of jeans stood in front of him, something to keep him entertained while he waited.

"Can I help you, sir?" The barista, in her twenties, with bleach-blonde hair and a nose ring, asked once the other guy had moved away.

"Large coffee, black, large tea, black, and two pumpkin cream cheese muffins."

The girl blinked at him. "Do you need another minute?"

Oh, crap. He hadn't said the order aloud. "Sorry. Large coffee, black, large tea, black, and two pumpkin cream cheese muffins."

"For here?"

He nodded.

She finished ringing the order. "That's eleven forty-one."

He passed her a ten-dollar bill and dropped a toonie, into her hand, waving her off when she tried to give him his less than a dollar change.

He balanced the plates in one hand and the stacked drinks in the other as he made his way over to Jaden. He set the muffins on the table and handed her the tea.

She glanced at him. "*Milk? Sugar?*"

He dropped himself into the chair opposite her. "Get it yourself."

She clicked her teeth, snatched her tea, and stalked over to the little bar holding the condiments. He watched as she went, pausing to check out the cute guy again. He seemed like someone who would be a top, though, so that put him off-limits. Jaden didn't say anything else until she plunked her petite body into the chair and her eyes narrowed like she had been reading his thoughts.

"*We need to figure out which other girls might have been there with Emily.*" He took a sip of his coffee, hissing as it burned his tongue.

"*I know. I haven't been able to reach Emily, waking or sleeping, since this morning.*" She picked at her muffin. "*I think she's shutting herself off at the moment.*"

His stomach lurched. He knew by instinct what she meant. This poor kid shut herself off from Jaden, not sharing whatever current horror she endured. It made him want to punch something. "*Did she give you any images or names last night?*"

She shook her head. "*Just the visuals. Pretty good for a scared kid.*"

"*I think this perp has a type. Emily looks an awful lot like Marissa.*" He took another sip of his coffee as Jaden typed away on her keyboard. "*Are there any other girls around that age who are blonde in the missing persons' files?"*

She turned the computer to face him. She'd already read his mind and done a search. A slide show of five other girls, similar to Marissa and Emily, flashed across the screen. *"Missing and unsolved, all in the last three-and-a-half years."*

"Six girls, including Emily. Why the heck has no one noticed?" Anger rose in his chest. Seven little girls in three-and-a-half years, and Marissa was the first one to get any media attention. The first someone cared enough about to go out and search for her, to have someone beg for her return on the television. Cop or not it just didn't sit right with him. He sipped of his coffee and nibbled on his muffin, while Jaden went through the information.

"Seems like one could be a parental abduction. Let's take her off the list. The first one was three-and-a-half years ago. Then a second a year and three months later, the third a year later, and the forth nine months after that. Emily was reported missing six months ago, and four days ago Marissa."

Based on this timeline, the perpetrator was accelerating. He stole Emily and the girl before her in a three-month span, which could mean there would be another kidnapping sooner rather than later. *"He's devolving."*

"Ya think?" Jaden's attitude flashed. When she got frustrated with a case, she oozed more sarcasm than usual.

He countered. *"Down, girl. I'm not the enemy, remember?"*

"Whatever." She took a large bite of her muffin and dragged the computer in front of her, clicking away.

He'd been dismissed for the time being. Bringing out his phone, he texted Ruth, asking her to pull the files on the girls. Knowing everything about them, their backgrounds, last known addresses, where they were last seen, the works, it would give him a place to start.

All of the sudden, Jaden froze. Panic radiated from her. Not words, but pure emotions hit him square in the chest.

No. It couldn't be.

Jaden choked down the bite of muffin she'd been chewing on.

She closed the lid of her laptop, stuffed it in the case, and hurried out of the coffee shop. The pain she projected left him surprised no one else stopped to stare at her.

He grabbed their drinks, leaving the half-eaten muffins on the table. He shoved past a dark-haired woman going into the coffee shop as he ran after Jaden.

He found her curled in a ball in the backseat of her SUV. Tears streaked her face, her heavy eye makeup running into a mess. He climbed in, opening his arms to her, and she buried her face in his chest. He patted the back of her head, smoothing her jet-black bob. His heart broke a tiny bit. He could count on one hand the number of times he'd seen Jaden this upset. Whatever she felt, it was bad and had changed his crass, flippant partner into a scared kid herself.

"What happened?"

She didn't answer.

"*Jay, talk to me. What happened?*"

A wave of sorrow hit him. "*Emily. I....*"

Images flashed into his brain. He could make out the dark figure of a man...and the chain. He could feel the squeeze around his neck and her final thought of how she wanted her mommy.

Chapter Two

Jaden snapped the images from him. He felt as destroyed as Jaden appeared. The child she had been talking to this morning had just been killed. He had no doubts she had seen—had felt— Emily's murder. Jaden prevented him from experiencing most of the images from him, her talent scared her as much as her ability to literally see the world through someone else's eyes, and she'd just seen the world through the eyes of a nine-year-old as she was murdered. That wasn't something she would forget with ease.

"We'll catch him, Jay, I promise." She nodded into his chest. *"We'll catch him."*

The tears stopped, and she clung to him. He tried to think comforting and protective thoughts. Cameron reached behind the seats and into the hatchback trunk. He felt around with one hand until he located a go-bag. He pulled it into the backseat and opened it, digging around until he found the pack of baby wipes he knew Jaden kept in there.

"Here, clean your face," he offered gently. She pulled away and took the wipes, cleaning off the streaks of makeup. *"Why don't I take you home?"*

"No." Jaden replied soft and distant, like she needed to try and rebuild the walls shattered by Emily's violent last images.

"Jaden, you're in no condition to work. Go home, get some

rest, and I'll go to the office and start working the files of the other girls. Maybe I can find a common thread."

"No."

"Give me the keys, Jaden." He held out his hand. She shook her head. He persisted. After a brief stare-off, she handed him the keys to the SUV. She stayed silent in the backseat until he pulled into the underground parking at her swanky condo building in the trendy Church and Wellesley Village neighborhood. He parked in her assigned spot.

"Come in with me."

He hesitated. It would be the first time in their two-year-plus partnership Cameron had been inside her condo. When they worked from home, they used his place, as he had ample parking and a large second room that doubled as an office. Jaden had always claimed her place was too small for them to work well. One more glance at his partner and he caved. She needed him.

He followed her inside, carrying her laptop to the elevator, then to her condo on the fifteenth floor. The thick carpeting muffled their footsteps as they made their way down the long hallway to her apartment. Jaden unlocked her door and showed him in.

The glass walls and the views of steel and concrete of downtown Toronto were in sharp contrast to the rest of the space. Warm and inviting, rich colors on the walls, cozy throw rugs and plush furniture—nothing at all like the condo he'd pictured Jaden living in. He'd always figured it would be more industrial somehow, reflecting the punk rocker in her rather than a down-home country girl.

She flicked a switch on the wall, and a soft, almost electrical humming filled his ears. *"Stops me from accidentally projecting and, more importantly, blocks everyone else out. You'll get used to it after a few minutes."*

"Can you hear me?" He tested her.

"Yes, of course." She raised an eyebrow at his question.

"How, if the noise blocks people?"

"I want to hear you. Sit, I'll be back in a few." She

disappeared into a room off the tiny office alcove. He explored the space. No TV in the condo, but a large sound system with a massive bass sat in a corner. Five bookshelves stuffed to the point of overflowing dominated the room. Volumes that didn't fit teetered next to them. Yesterday's newspaper sat haphazardly piled on one corner of the coffee table, a mug and a plate with leftover crumbs sat next to it. Grabbing the dishes, he dumped them into the sink, on top of the handful of items piled in there. The blanket on the large couch lay thrown over one end as though someone had pushed it off when they woke. It seemed Jaden hadn't been expecting company. He sat on the smaller couch, sensing she preferred the larger one.

The screen separating the living room from another space opened, and Jaden stepped out. Gone were the trendy skinny jeans and knee-high boots, with the ripped tank top with some indie band name and covered by a stylish jacket. In their place, she wore a pair of plaid PJ pants and a shirt three sizes too big splashed with the logo of some hockey team he had never heard of before.

Jaden dropped onto the big couch and grabbed the blanket, wrapping it around herself. Without the makeup and stylish clothes, he'd never seen his strong and attitude-filled partner look so vulnerable, so young, so much smaller than her five-foot frame. Most people pegged her at much older than her real age. Old-soul, people often called her. Her bright green eyes stood out against her too-pale skin and black hair, giving her a haunted appearance.

Feelings of despair and most of all loneliness encircled him, like someone punched him in the stomach. He was always Jaden's protector, the one who carried the badge and took care of her at all costs. In this instant, he felt utterly helpless, unable to save her from the images burned into her mind. Jaden wasn't saying anything either, so he didn't think she even knew she was projecting to him. Maybe they were just so tuned into each other's brainwaves that he was getting more from her than she meant to share, a curse of being such a powerful telepath.

"*Do you want me to stay and work the case files from here?*"
A sense of relief washed over him.

"*Only if you want,*" she replied, in her usual standoffish
manner. She could be so stubborn, but she was projecting enough
so he knew the truth.

"*Let me call Ruth, see if she can digitize the files and e-mail
them to me. Can I use your computer?*"

Jaden nodded, which Cameron took as a yes. He dialed Ruth
and requested the info. She pulled the files while he was on the
phone with her and sent the four digital ones. The other two she
would have to pull and scan, which would take a while.

Cameron logged onto Jaden's desktop and used her laser
printer to run off the files. He even found department-issue file
folders to organize them in and returned to his spot on the small
couch in the living room. Jaden still had the blanket wrapped
around her, and she ignored him as she pounded on the keys of
her laptop. Cameron spread out on the coffee table as best he
could, keeping Emily's file unopened and hidden under the other
ones. He wasn't ready to read it yet, and he felt Jaden wouldn't be
either.

He gleaned as much information as possible from the other
two. Both were blonde girls; the first went missing in June 2010.
Her name was Olivia, aged seven but looked older. She had been
taken into foster care from a crack-head mother. Separated from
an older sister, Olivia bounced around a lot. She had been in
fifteen or so homes in four years. There'd been reports of sexual
abuse by two of the foster families during that time. She was
always running away, trying to find her older sister. Christ. No
wonder her disappearance went under the radar.

The next one was also a foster kid. Jody had been eight,
blonde hair. Placed in a care home after running away from four
foster homes and showing unsocial behavior. There were notes
from a file in sex crimes. Abused by her mother's boyfriends from
the time she was three to the time she was six...until social
services had taken her away. It took the care home a week to
report her missing. Another throwaway kid.

"*They're not throwaways.*" Jaden's sharp thought interrupted his stream of consciousness. She had once told him she liked just listening to him while he was in cop mode. It gave her a direction in which to focus.

"*I know they're not, but that's how the initial investigators treated them.*"

Jaden fell silent, focusing on her laptop. "*What about Emily?*"

"*Are you sure you want me to go there? I can call Ruth and see how the other files are coming.*" He didn't want to overwhelm her with Emily just yet. What she had seen would be too raw, too fresh in her memory to be good for her.

"*Tell me her story, Cam.*"

He opened the file. Emily's parents had been killed in a car accident a year and a half ago. They'd been in their forties when she came along, and an elderly grandmother was deemed an unfit guardian, so she'd entered into foster care. She'd been in one of the same homes Olivia had been in. One of the ones where Olivia had reported abuse.

Emily had reported the same.

Christ.

How in the hell had the system let them keep kids after that? Emily's report was almost identical to Olivia's. He didn't bother reading past the first few paragraphs, deciding to skip the repeat. After the abuse, they'd switched her foster homes, and every chance she got she ran to the senior's apartment her grandmother lived in. Her grandmother often didn't report Emily was there. The original investigators just wrote it off as Emily running away, even though her grandmother made the police report. There was no mention of the foster family even noticing she was missing.

"*We need to look at whoever deals with child sex crimes in the Special Crimes Unit.*"

He raised an eyebrow at her. "*How did you get that?*"

"*Marissa was abused by a grandfather, Emily and Olivia by foster families, Jody by her mother's boyfriends. That's their common thread."*

"There is nothing in Marissa's file about abuse." Cameron reached for the file he knew was tucked away in her laptop case.

"Her mother started to file a report, but she never finished the process. She thinks Marissa ran away over it, and it's her fault Marissa is missing."

"You didn't say anything before." He felt a bit lied to. Jaden had held back a key piece of information that may have been pertinent to the case.

"It didn't seem important until now. Who took the first reports?"

He studied the reports from Emily, Jody, and Olivia. *"Sergeant Matthew Meincke for Emily and Jody. For Olivia...."* His stomach twisted into knots when he read the name. *"...Sergeant Matthew Meincke."*

"Oh God, you don't think?" she whispered.

He glanced at Jaden. That was exactly what he thought, and she knew it.

"There are only a handful of investigators in sex crimes. We need the other files first, and we need to find who Marissa's mother talked to in sex crimes, if it made it that far." His heart beat a bit faster, but he tried to stay calm, not wanting to reveal his feelings to her. He brought his block higher, hiding the rest of his racing thought process. Another cop—another brother—they were talking about. They needed to be cautious about what they were alleging. Especially Jaden. She'd become too emotionally embroiled already. Her crass attitude might be very dangerous, and they needed to tread with care until they were sure Meincke was a viable suspect. It had to be a coincidence; there was no way one of their own could do this. No way.

As if on cue, his phone vibrated. He checked it—an e-mail from Ruth with the other files. He went to the computer, printed everything off, and organized it. He could feel Jaden's impatience as he put everything together. He wanted to make sure he had everything correct.

He sat on the couch and flipped through the oldest file. He

brought his block down so she could thought-monitor. Three-and-a-half years ago, a pretty eight-year-old named Grace disappeared. Her story mirrored the others. Abuse, foster home, and more abuse. The name on the second abuse report was Sergeant Matthew Meincke. Waves of nausea rolled over Cameron, and he recognized the feelings not as his own but coming from Jaden. He grabbed the final file. Her name was Taylor, tiny for a nine-year-old, blonde hair. He didn't bother reading more than the barebones of her details—foster kid, abused. He went to the abuse report and skimmed the details. Before he finished reading, Jaden bolted off the coach and made a beeline for the bathroom. He followed her and held her long bangs as she threw up.

Chapter Three

The low-rise apartment building where Marissa's mother lived looked like a hundred other subsidized housing units in the city. Brick, white trim, two-and-a-half story walk-up. He parked Jaden's SUV in front of the building.

"*I'm here.*"

"*Okay. I'll be listening,*" she replied, sounding farther away than usual, being in her condo downtown, and not next to him in the car.

It wasn't unusual for her to be on the other side of the glass when he questioned someone at the station. She could get a better read if she kept her distance and stayed more objective than sitting in the room listening to the perp and reading his mind. Then she would send him her impressions, which helped lead his questioning, clean and simple. Made it seem like he was an investigator with a hell of an intuition rather than a regular cop with a telepath guiding his questioning. When he did interviews with victims or their families, she was usually right there with him in the room. She had a gift for comforting people and seeing through their pain to the truth, whether they wanted her to see it or not.

Today, however, the visions from this morning haunted her. She needed to stay home and rest. He could tell from the sheer number of emotions rolling off of her she wasn't fit to be in public. Not yet, anyway.

The questioning would be rather cut-and-dry today. Get the name of the officer she reported Marissa's assault to. If it was Meincke, then they would go to Internal Affairs to ask for help investigating, just to cover all the possible bases. If not, they might find themselves helping out with a few sexual assault cases until they got to know Meincke a bit better, and Jaden could get a solid read from him.

He rang the buzzer to Cindy Preston's apartment. He had been working with Cindy since Marissa disappeared. A young, single mom with a deadbeat ex who took off before Marissa's birth. His parents had taken Cindy and her baby in after her parents kicked her out. They lived there during Cindy's high school and college as she studied to become a practical nurse. They moved into this apartment four years ago, but Grandma and Grandpa still watched Marissa while Cindy worked, until, it appeared, Marissa told Cindy her grandfather was touching her. At least that explained the sudden change in Cindy's behavior. Something about the abrupt routine change had bugged him from the beginning.

"Hello?" Cindy said through the intercom.

"Cindy? It's Detective Olsen with the Toronto Police Department. May I come in?"

"Oh yes, of course. Apartment five."

The door buzzed a moment later, and he took the stairs two at a time to the top floor. The building stank of cooking smells and stale cigarette smoke, but Cindy's apartment smelt fresh and appeared immaculate.

"Hi, Cindy," he said as she let him into the apartment. "I'm sorry to bother you."

Blonde and petite, just like her daughter, Cindy seemed exhausted, dressed in a pair of scrubs with teddy bears on them. "You're not bothering me. I just have to leave for work soon. Do you have any news on Marissa?"

He would have thought it odd that Cindy was going to work so soon after Marissa's disappearance, but she had explained she didn't have any sick or vacation time at the moment. Work offered her three days off before she had to return. Jaden confirmed, as any parent would be, Cindy was heartbroken—she couldn't stay home and had nothing to do with her daughter's disappearance.

"Not yet. I just came by to ask a few more questions. I won't take much of your time." He kept his voice soft and non-threatening. "Why don't we sit down?"

Cindy showed him into the living room, filled with older hand-me-down furniture, and children's toys neatly tucked into the corner, waiting for their owner to return. She sat on the couch, and he took the chair on instinct, giving him a separation and giving him in a better position to watch her. He might not be able to read someone's mind but was damn good at reading body language.

"What do you need to know, Detective?" She held her hands in a tight clasp on her lap.

"You can call me Cameron," he reminded her.

She nodded and stared downward at the floor.

"Cindy, I'm here to ask you about the report you started a couple of months ago. I know Marissa told you her grandfather was touching her, and you went to the police to report the abuse."

She regarded him, pain and sadness in her eyes. "Yes, I.... How did you know?"

"One of the officers remembered you came in to make a report." He felt guilty about lying to her, but it was the only way to explain how they knew the information. "They couldn't remember all of the details."

"Oh." Cindy remained quiet for a long moment. "Do you think it's important to the investigation?"

"It could be."

Cindy chewed her bottom lip. "It was about five months or so ago. I found red marks on the private spots of her dolls." She blinked away tears. "At first, I just thought she was coloring on her dolls, so I yelled at her. That's when she told me she was making her dollies look like her."

"Poor kid," Jaden said. He gave her a mental push to be quiet. He needed to pay attention to Cindy, not to her.

"I asked who hurt her. At first, when she told me it was her Grandpa Fred, I didn't believe her. I mean, he'd always been so good to us. Then she started in with the details, stuff no kid should know. I remember once my ex's cousin saying her uncle was a dirty bastard. I contacted her and asked her, she confirmed it and I knew it was true. That asshole touched my baby." She glanced away for a moment, blinking, struggling with more tears. "I went to the police station and filled out the report. They wanted me to go downtown to Special Crimes Unit. I was going to, really. But when I found daycare and a babysitter rather than give her back to her grandparents, Fred figured out Marissa had told me. He promised to never hurt her again. He said reporting it to the police would be too traumatic for her, dredge it all up again. I thought he was right, so I let it go."

He nodded and took some notes on her story. Flawed as fuck, but he believed her. It never made it past the initial reporting officer. He thought for sure their perp had something to do with Sex Crimes, he stopped himself from sighing with relief—maybe the perp was just in Child Protective Services, all the other kids were in foster care.

"Ask her if anyone from Sex Crimes followed up."

"Did anyone from Special Crimes unit ever follow up?" he asked her. "Maybe they called or dropped in for a visit"

Cindy frowned, thinking hard. "Now that you mention it, yes, some officers did come by about a month after I made the initial report. I invited them in but explained I didn't want to pursue the complaint further."

"Do you know who it was? I mean which detective, so I can contact them."

"Yes. Hang on a second. They left a card." Cindy stood and disappeared into the apartment. She returned two minutes later, carrying a card, and handed it to him.

It read: *"Detective Leann Steel, Special Crimes Unit"* and her office number. He jotted the information down on his notepad and returned the card to her.

"Thank you for all of your help, Cindy. The second I know anything, you'll know." He stood and went to the door.

"Thank you very much, Cameron." She seemed so lost he reached out and hugged her. Jaden was so much better at these things than him. "Thank you." Cindy pulled away fighting off more tears.

"No problem." He patted her on the arm and gave her another smile before he left the apartment.

"*Really, you hugged her? You are going soft on me, Cam,*" Jaden teased as he made his way to the car.

"*Yeah, well, she looked like she needed it. No dice on Meincke, though.*" He unlocked the SUV and climbed inside.

"*Wow, you are the most unobservant ogre I have ever met.*"

He swore he could hear her clicking her teeth at him. "*Cindy said they stopped by, meaning two officers. What do you want to bet Steele and Meincke are partners in Sex Crimes?*"

"*There's only one way to find out. Let me call Ruth. I'll get back to you.*"

"*Sure.*" She retreated into her own mind.

Cameron popped his Bluetooth in and dialed Ruth's direct line.

"Hello, sweet pea, how did the interview with Cindy go?"

"Good. Listen, I need you to do me a favor, unofficially."

Ruth, their admin assistant and magic maker, made a noise through her nose "Go ahead, tiger."

"Find out if Leann Steele and Matthew Meincke are partners in Sex Crimes and, if they are, which shift they work." He pulled into the main flow of traffic and headed toward his partner's apartment.

"Unofficially?"

"Uh-huh."

Ruth sighed. "Then what?"

He paused for a second, thinking about what could be their way in. "If they do, then pull some files they need help on, so we can offer to consult."

"What about Marissa?"

"Trust me, Ruth."

"Always, sweetie. I'll hit your cell when I know more." She disconnected.

He made his way through the early rush-hour to Jaden's, missing the worst of the traffic nightmare. One thing he hated about living in this city, the traffic was hell most of the time. He tried to raise her at a red light, twice, but got nothing. He let himself into Jaden's underground garage, then into her condo. As he went to call her name, he found her passed out on the couch, fast asleep.

Damn, he didn't know the last time he saw Jaden actually sleep. The visions of Emily must have been a lot harder on her than he'd imagined.

Jaden seemed uncomfortable on the couch, one arm half dangling off the edge. Slipping out of his suit jacket and tie, he hung them on the back of a chair, and stopped to roll up his sleeves. She moaned and turned awkwardly. He couldn't leave her there, not when the bed was just a few steps away. Cameron went through the sliding screen and into the bedroom crossing the small space to turn down the snow-white covers. Being in his partner's bedroom made him feel a little self-conscious, knowing she could lay there within arm's reach. His body responded to the idea of what he could do with her in bed. He pushed it all aside and returned to the couch, lifting Jaden into his arms. She felt so light, he guessed she weighted a hundred pounds dripping wet. He could bench pressed twice that amount at the gym.

She snuggled into his chest and sighed. So trusting. Jaden always kept parts of herself locked away, but for the first time he believed he might be getting to know her. He carried her into her bedroom and laid her down, her tiny frame seeming so lost on the huge king-sized bed. He tucked her in and settled in the living room, leaving the screen open just enough in case she needed him.

He studied the files, trying to glean more information from them. Any links other than the Sex Crimes Unit. Emily and Olivia shared the same foster family as Taylor, where all three girls reported abuse. It was enough of a link they had to investigate it as well.

He glanced at his watch, close to five. He tried his contact at Child Protective Services but got a voicemail telling him he had missed her. Damn. He left a message for her to give him a call in the morning.

He looked at the address of the foster home. Way out in the suburbs. He checked the map on his phone—almost two hours in traffic to get there even with rush hour starting to peter out. He didn't want to interview anyone without Jaden.

His cell rang. *Ruth.*

"You know how hard it is to find out *unofficially* who is partnered with whom in Sex Crimes?" She sounded amused.

"Nope. But you did it, right?"

"Of course. Steele and Meincke have been partners in Sex Crimes for the past three and a half years."

Damn, the first abduction happened then. Not what he wanted to hear. "Okay."

"Meincke is technically a Provincial Police officer. He's working for Sex Crimes here as the Special Child Unit covers most of this half of Ontario, not just Toronto. The department has about twenty-five investigators. He was a Sex Crime investigator based in Ottawa before he got this job. Divorced twice. Two sons, sixteen and fourteen, they live with their mother in Ottawa. Working on his last known address, current property holdings, and any current love interests."

He let out a low whistle. "You got all this unofficially?"

"What can I say? One of the sex crimes admin assistants is a chatter box, especially when you bring her a box of chocolates."

"How much is this going to cost me, and do we have the room in the expense account?"

Ruth laughed. "Don't worry about it. You still want me to pull some files?"

"Yup."

"Okay. I'll send whatever they have that looks half-decent and is digital. I'll digitize the paper files tomorrow and send them off to you."

"You're amazing, Ruth. Buy yourself a treat."

"Don't worry, I already did." She ended the call.

He pulled out all the files he had at Jaden's place, and re-read every word of them, searching for clues. Based on the only basic of reports so many of the files had only gotten a cursory glance from the initial investigating officers.

His neck ached from hunching over his partner's coffee table. His stomach growled, and he glanced at the clock on the stove, well after six. He hadn't eaten since the granola bar and half the muffin earlier this morning. No wonder he was hungry.

He cleared the files, stacking them on Jaden's desk in her tiny alcove of an office, then he peeked in on her. Still asleep. He went to her kitchen, hunting for some take-out menus. Instead, he found fully stocked cupboards and fridge and set about making dinner.

Jaden wandered out of the bedroom, rubbing her eyes as he dumped the pot of steaming potatoes into the strainer in the sink. *"What time is it?"*

"Just after seven."

"Oh crap, how long was I asleep for?"

"About four hours."

"Oh. Dinner smells good. Did you make enough for me?" She sat on one of the high stools at the counter, appearing even more exhausted than she did this morning.

"No, I cooked using your food and only made enough for me."

She wrinkled her nose in the most adorable way. *"Thank you."*

She wasn't acting like herself, which worried him. However, when he slid a heaping plate of food in front of her, she brightened—so that was something.

As they ate, Cameron filled her in on the details of the investigation. They spent some time reviewing the two files Ruth had sent them, to see if either of them would be a good cover-case for them to use. They weren't.

Jaden's energy faded fast after dinner. Once he finished the cleanup he suggested he should go.

"*Do you have to?*" The suggestion seemed to panic Jaden.

"*Why?*"

"*I don't know.*" She shivered. "*I just don't want to be alone. Not tonight. Something tells me I shouldn't be.*"

"*I'll sleep on the couch,*" he offered, struggling to block his thoughts from her. He wanted this more than anything. Even though he knew it wouldn't lead anywhere. The idea of Jaden inviting him to stay had his heart pumping. "*Just let me get my go-bag out of your SUV.*"

They both kept a go-bag in her car. He never knew where he might end up on an investigation, and where he would be when it was time to crash for a few hours.

"*It's okay. You can have my bed. I'll take the couch. You won't fit very well.*"

Although the larger couch was big enough for her, one glance at it told him it was far too tiny for his six-foot-two, two-hundred-and-fifty pound frame. "*I won't take your bed away from you, Jaden.*"

"*You just admitted the couch was too small for you.*"

Damn telepath. "*I've slept on worse.*"

She clicked her teeth at his comment. "*You don't have to. Take my bed. I promise it's nice and comfy.*"

"*No, Jaden, you need a good night's sleep.*"

"*Fine, then share it with me. It's a king size, plenty of space for both of us. Besides, we've shared before.*"

Hotel beds on an investigation were different than their personal spaces, though. He didn't need the temptation of having her asleep next to him without the threat of work interrupting them at a moment's notice.

She crossed her arms and tapped her foot, and he knew he had lost.

"*I'll go get my go-bag.*" He walked out of her apartment, cursing.

Why did he always cave to her? He retrieved his duffle and returned upstairs. Water running in the bathroom told him where to find Jaden as he returned to the condo. While he waited for the bathroom to be free, he pulled out a pair of PJ pants and his shaving kit. He hung the spare suit in the closet, hoping it would de-wrinkle somewhat by the morning.

Jaden emerged from the bathroom, wearing a different set of PJ's. The top declared Princesses needed their beauty sleep and the waistband of the pants were rolled down so they rested just below the bony outcropping of her hips. "*Bathroom's yours.*" She crawled onto the opposite side of the bed in which he'd tucked her into earlier.

He changed and brushed his teeth then went into the bedroom. Jaden had already curled under the covers, clutching the blue hippopotamus named David to her chest. She had once told him a childhood friend had given her the hippo. He protected her while she slept at night.

He double-checked the door was locked, turning off the lights in the apartment as he went.

"*Shut the doors to the closet. I don't want the monsters to get out.*" Jaden sounded closer to sleep than awake. "*The blinds, too.*"

"*Sure, get some sleep. I'm not going anywhere, I promise.*"

"*Thank you.*"

He flicked the final light off and settled next to his partner. He worried about her, but sooner rather than later, he slipped into a deep sleep.

Chapter Four

*H*e needed a flashlight to search this cave properly. He inched along the wall, his head a bit fuzzy. *How did I get here?*

He checked his belt, and the flashlight appeared there. Flicking it on, the beam revealed nothing spectacular, rocks and the scurry of a mouse at the edge of the light. He hoped it was a just a mouse. He ventured farther, feeling compelled to keep going.

The farther he got into the cave, the warmer he became. Not colder as he expected. A few drops of water dripped from the stalactites. Well, that was something. Bears didn't sleep in caves with running or dripping water, he was sure of it.

He rounded the tunnel into an open cavern, and bears were the least of his worries. Cameron blinked, and then blinked again, and he clued in that he must be dreaming—he *hoped* he was dreaming.

Lying in one corner of the cave were dragons. Two, actually. A large green one with a yellow underbelly and dark green spines, and a tiny black one. Every time the green one breathed out, fire flared a good five feet from his nostrils, just brushing over the other much smaller dragon tucked under his wing. The smaller one had wicked silver spikes running down her backside. They both appeared to be asleep.

Cam backed out of the cave. The last thing he wanted to do was awaken two very mean dragons.

He had almost inched out of the area when a low rumble of a voice reverberated off the walls. "How dare you enter my cave."

Turning around, Cam shook as he watched the larger of the two dragons getting to his feet, careful not to disturb the tiny black one. Somehow he knew the larger green dragon protected the smallest of the pair. "I'm sorry," he whispered. "I didn't mean to."

The green one turned and breathed fire on the smaller dragon. He seemed to be warming her, and then he stalked toward Cam. "Who are you? How did you get in here?"

For whatever reason, a talking dragon didn't seem unusual to him. "I don't know. I just came here. I'm sorry." His eyes darted to the exit, mentally calculating if he could make it there without getting roasted.

"How did you get here? No one can come here." The dragon roared and stomped his feet, fire flying from his nostrils, hitting the wall of the cave next to him.

"I don't know. I just appeared here." His repeated explanation seemed to upset the dragon further.

"You cannot just appear here. It does not work like that. You can only come here if I bring you here." The dragon came a foot from him, sniffing him from head to toe.

He shook with fear. One wrong move and he would be toast. "I'll go. I promise I won't cause any trouble," he offered.

The dragon laughed. "Don't be silly. Now that you're here you might as well be my midnight snack. I was feeling a bit hungry."

"You can't eat him, Paul." Jaden's panicked voice filled the cave.

The green dragon turned to look at the black dragon hurrying toward them. She stood on her hind legs, and Cameron could see she wasn't all black. A green starburst the exact color of Jaden's eyes splashed across the dragon's chest.

"You should be resting," Paul admonished.

It made perfect sense to him the black dragon with the green star was Jaden.

"I was cold," she explained.

"Go lie down. I'll be there once I take care of our guest." He tried to give her a small push with his tail, and she reacted by raising her spikes.

"I told you, you can't eat him!" Her deadly spikes swished to and fro with menace.

The green dragon sat on his haunches. "I wasn't going to eat him. I was going to show him to the door." He gestured toward the opening to the cave with his shorter forelegs, doing his best to appear innocent.

Cam watched in amazement as Jaden, the dragon, grew in size until she towered over the green one. "Do not lie to me, Paul! You were going to eat him." Smoke curled from her nostrils.

"Now hang on a moment. He's an unwanted visitor here. We cannot have people like him here, luv. They're dangerous." Paul, the green dragon, stared at Jaden.

"He's not dangerous. I brought him here." She shuffled closer to him, spreading out her wings to shield him.

"How could you bring him here?" Fire shot from the green dragon's nostrils. He flinched and leaned in close to Jaden, convinced they were both going to be barbequed.

She fluttered out her wing, protecting him from the fire. "I didn't mean to bring Cameron here, Paul. It was an accident."

"Cameron. He's Cameron?" He reached out with his broad green wing and lifted Jaden's black one. "So, you're Cameron."

"Yes." He hid behind the black dragon's large hind leg, protecting himself from Paul.

The green dragon leaned in a few inches, regarding him with large yellow eyes. "Well then, why didn't you say so?"

Jaden ruffled her wings, and slowly she decreased her size to normal. She nuzzled Cam with her snout. "I'm glad you stayed."

"Dragons?" This all seemed a bit much. He felt calm, but the logical part of his brain screamed something wasn't right, this wasn't real.

Jaden smiled, or at least he thought it was a smile—her teeth were large and pointy. "It's my natural dream guide. Come."

She folded her wing out and picked him up, tucking him into her side. She moved to where Paul had settled, waiting for her.

Paul sniffed Jaden. "I suppose you want him to sleep with us."

"He'll be cold."

He huffed, smoke curling out of his nostrils. "Fine, we'll sleep in a proper bed, then."

Cameron felt woozy then he blinked. The dragons were gone and he stood on a misty plane, next to a man who he knew by instinct was Paul. He was blond to Cam's brown, tall, but not quite as tall as him. Lean, with a swimmer's body and blue eyes. His mouth went dry—exactly the kind of guy he went for, a bit older, mature but still very sexy.

"Really?" Jaden turned and regarded Paul. "You hate sleeping in our human bodies...." The rest of the sentence didn't register on his brain. Instead, he stared open-mouthed at Jaden. At least he assumed the woman was Jaden.

Gone was the short black bob and stylish punk appearance. She wore her hair long, well past her shoulders, and wavy, like it would be so soft to touch. The long white dress she had on seemed to float off of her. She appeared older somehow, with laugh lines around her eyes and her smile easier, more at peace.

"Sorry, Cameron." She spoke to him, not just in her mind voice but actual words came flowing from her mouth. He blinked at her, stunned. "I forgot how different I look here."

"You're beautiful." The words tumbled from his mouth before he could think. The thoughts of Paul were lost as he stared at his gorgeous partner, his body reacting to seeing her in such a natural and beautiful state.

She blushed and glanced toward Paul. "Are you sure you won't sleep with us?"

"You don't need me, luv." He reached out and tucked her hair behind her ear. "You have your own protector tonight, in the world of the sleeping and in the world of the waking." Paul stared at him, hard. "Take good care of my girl."

A soft breeze whisper past Cam, and when he turned to ask Paul a question, he had disappeared. He stared at Jaden. "That's your lover?"

"No. He's just a friend…it's complicated. Come on." She held out her hand, and he took it. She led him through a door that just appeared leading into a swanky hotel room.

"*How did you do that*?" he asked. "*Jay*?" Then he spoke aloud. "Jay."

"What?" She turned to face him. "Oh, I can't read your mind here. You actually have to talk to me."

"Why not?"

"Because this is Dreamworld, Cameron, and we're in a world of our creating." A second door opened, revealing a huge bed. Covered with pillows and blankets, inviting as though they could sink into it and never move again. "Whatever you want in this world will happen."

He wanted the room darker, more romantic. All of the sudden, the room dimmed and candles appeared on the tables. "Like that?" He glanced at her. *Is this what she wants?*

She brought him to a room holding one bed. He just had a feeling this had been what she was hinting at.

She moved closer to him. She stood taller in Dreamworld, but still she raised herself onto her tippy-toes. "Exactly like that." Her mouth was a few inches from his lips.

"Jaden." He tried to warn her off, but it didn't matter, her soft lips pressed against his. His lips parted, and she slipped her tongue in, and they were full-on kissing. *I'm kissing Jaden.*

The thought sank into his mind, and he pulled away, as though he had been burned by Paul's dragon fire. "We can't do this."

"This is Dreamworld, Cameron, we can do whatever we want." She moved in for a kiss, her fingers sliding down his chest and under the T-shirt he wore. She skimmed over his hard abs and higher, pinching his nipples.

"If you don't stop right now, Jay, I'm not going to be able to stop myself."

"I don't want you to stop, Cameron. I've wanted you for so long. Don't deny you want me as well." Her soft, angelic voice drew him in. "You're not as good at blocking me as you think you are."

Cameron pulled her close, already half-hard at the thought. It was true, there were times when he'd wished they could be more than police partners, but he'd thought he had always blocked those feelings from her. "What about work and rules?"

She held a finger to his lips, silencing him. "This is Dreamworld, Cam, no rules and no real-world consequences."

He slid his hands over her back. Finding the top of her zipper, he pulled it down, and she smiled at him with a glint in her eyes. With the zipper undone all the way, she stepped away from him and let the dress fall away, revealing her perfect body. She seemed curvier here, a little more mature. He ached from the sight of her. He cupped her round and perky breasts, his rough thumb massaging the nipple until she moaned.

"More," she demanded, moving away just enough so her fingers could grasp the hem of his T-shirt. He helped her pull it off then his PJ pants hit the floor, leaving them both naked.

She gasped once his full manhood came into view. "God, you're gorgeous, so big."

He grinned at her—he wasn't the biggest in the world, but he was happy with what he had. She stroked him, his foreskin sliding over the head of his penis and making him groan with pleasure.

"Come on, let's move this somewhere more comfortable." She pulled him backward, and he took over, lifting her and carrying them to the plush bed. They fell together, landing with the softest thud, his body covering hers.

Cam kissed her, his hands trailing downward, rubbing against her nipples. He moved lower over her flat stomach, searching for his ultimate prize. As he brushed over the hard nub at the top of her wet heat, she panted. With each stroke, Jaden squirmed beneath him, moving her hips to make greater contact with his palm.

"Shh...." he soothed. He slid his fingers even lower, just brushing against her slick entrance. "What do you want?"

"You. Any part of you."

He pressed one digit into her, gently, and withdrew.

"Please," she begged.

Thrusting inside again, he sought the spot that would give her the most pleasure. When he found it, she arched against him, asking for more.

He added a second one finger then twisted to tease her swollen clit with his thumb. "Do you like that?"

In response, she grasped his thick cock, moving the foreskin over the sensitive head. He opened his mouth in a silent gasp, burying his face into the pillow next to her head. As she stroked him in earnest, he swore into the pillow. "Do you like that?"

"Vixen."

She turned her head, and he kissed the skin on her neck then moved to lavish attention on one of her nipples. He sucked on her, hard, and she stopped stroking him, instead digging her fingers into his hair.

"That's it. I need you."

"How do you want me?" he asked, his voice heavy with need.

"Inside of me."

"When?"

"Now." She tugged at his hair, begging for more.

He found her sweet spot one last time with his fingers before he pulled them out. As he rolled away to get a condom, she stopped him.

"I need to get some protection."

"Dreamworld. There are no rules, no consequences, no condoms needed."

A deep growl resonated from his chest. Nothing between him and Jaden. He wanted this so much, he craved to feel her naked and open to him. He moved so he settled between her legs, and she guided him into her. Sliding inside, he took his time, pulling out a few inches before pushing in again.

They both let out a heady sigh as he settled into place. The second he started moving with a slow and steady rhythm, she moaned and soon begged for it hard, faster. He raised himself on his arms to give himself more leverage, and her hand went to her clit, working it over as he pistoned in and out of her.

"I'm already so close." Her head thrashed from side to side.

He increased the power behind his thrusts, his own release building, but he wanted to bring her there first. She gripped his cock like a vise a second before she threw back her head, the orgasm overtaking her body.

A few more pumps and he followed her over the edge. He kept moving for as long as he could until he collapsed onto her, leaning on his elbows so his full weight wasn't on her.

Their breath came in short pants, tendrils of pleasure still shooting through his body. He moved, and his softened cock slipped from her. He rolled over, and she followed, her head resting on his chest.

"You okay?" He ran his hands along her sweaty back.

"More than okay."

He closed his eyes, exhaustion taking hold of him.

"Sleep," she whispered. Her fingers drifted over his chest and down his arms.

His body drifted off onto a plane of oblivion, almost reaching the point of no return, and Paul's soft voice floated through his mind. "Are you sure you don't want him to remember this, Jay?"

"I'm sure, Paul. He can't remember anything."

"Very well, then."

A wave of pleasure carried him off to sleep.

Chapter Five

Cameron woke with a start, his heart pounding in his ears. The distant buzz of arousal and the stickiness in his boxers told him that, for the first time in about ten years, he'd had a proper wet dream.

Blinking his eyes open, he found himself in Jaden's bedroom, with his partner curled on her side next to him. One arm under her, and he cupped her breast. *Shit.*

Taking care not to wake her, he slid his hand out from under her. The second he freed his arm, he bolted into the bathroom, shutting the door behind him. He searched his brain. He couldn't remember what the dream had been about, but he had a sneaking suspicion it had something to do with Jaden. His heart thudded— he might care for his partner, but he couldn't think of her like that.

Cameron took a few calming breaths, allowing his heart rate to return to normal and the last buzzes of his release to leave his body. He glanced at his watch, just past eight. He hoped his contact from Child Protective Services returned his call first thing this morning.

He hit the shower, washing away the evidence of whatever happened last night. When he finished standing under the pounding water, he dried off, wrapped a towel around his waist, and padded into the bedroom to dig in his go-bag for a pair of clean underwear.

"*Well, that's a nice sight first thing in the morning.*" She sounded half-asleep.

He blushed—what the hell had gotten into Jaden? "*Morning.*"

Her eyes fluttered closed. "*What time is it?*"

"*Eight thirty-eight.*" He read the time off his watch.

She groaned. "*Do we have to go into the office today?*"

"*No. Waiting to hear back from CPS, then I want to head out and interview the foster family that housed some of the missing girls.*" He found a clean pair of boxer briefs and pulled them on under the towel.

"*When are you leaving?*"

"*Around ten.*"

"*Wake me in an hour or so.*" She rolled over and snuggled under the covers.

Dropping the towel, he strode to the closet. Damn, his suit was still wrinkled from the bag. "*Jay, where is your iron?*" She didn't answer other than to emit a soft snore. "*Jay, iron?*" Still nothing.

Cameron searched through the apartment, at last finding what he needed in the closet off the alcove office.

He set up the ironing board and pressed his dress shirt then slipped it on before he started on the pants, cursing when he made railroad tracks. His cell phone rang as he attempted to smooth them out.

"Olsen," he answered.

"Hi, Cameron, it's Paige Clark returning your call." His contact at CPS.

"Hi, thanks for returning my call." He set the iron on its side. "I needed some information on a foster home for an investigation."

"I'll see what I can do. What do you need?"

"Hang on, I need to grab the file." He grabbed Olivia's file from Jaden's desk then plunked into the comfortable desk chair.

"I need everything you have on a foster home run by Donald and Vanessa Jenkins. The address is out in Scarborough."

"Let me run a search." She said nothing for a long time, the silence punctuated by the clicking of her keyboard. "We don't have any active files for a Jenkins in that area."

"Try inactive files, or homes that have been shut down." Maybe after Emily's last report, someone listened and stopped placing foster kids there.

"Looks like the Jenkins's was a transition house. They only kept kids for a short period of time before they were more permanently placed. Their last foster kid left about nine month ago."

"Why?"

"No notes in the file. Just that they stopped receiving kids about a year ago."

"Who was the last kid they took in?" His heart raced. Emily had been placed with the Jenkins a year ago, before moving to a new home after she reported abuse there.

"I can't tell you that, Cam."

He hesitated then asked, "Was it Emily Knight?" He hoped to throw her off enough she would give him something else.

Paige paused. "Yes. How did you know?"

"I wish I could tell you, Paige. I need a list of every child that ever went through their doors."

"I can't. Not without a warrant. I shouldn't have even told you that. Besides, this was a transitional foster home. Do you have any idea how long the list is going to be? Sometimes they had kids for a night before they were moved on."

"'Which is exactly why I need a complete list, Paige. Start putting it together, you'll have a warrant by noon." He ended the call. He hated the need to go through the process of obtaining a warrant—Marissa might not have much time.

He dialed Ruth.

"I'm still working the files, Cameron," she said on answering the phone.

"I need a warrant."

"For what?"

"Records of the Jenkins's foster home. Three of the girls, Emily, Olivia, and Taylor, stayed there. I need the full records as it was a transitional home. I need to know if any of the other girls spent even an afternoon there."

"Do you have any idea how hard it is to get a warrant for that?" She paused. "No, of course you don't. I'll see what I can do."

"I need it by noon, Ruth."

"No promises." She disconnected.

He returned to ironing his suit only to find Jaden had already re-pressed the pants and was just finishing the jacket. His surprise must have registered with her.

"*Unobservant ogre,*" she teased.

"I was busy, thank you."

She smiled. She wore jeans and a trendy sweater long enough to be a dress, with her hair still wrapped in a towel. "*Here.*" She hung up the jacket. "*Get dressed. I need to finish getting ready.*"

He did, pulled his pants and suit jacket on, tucking it in and securing his gun to his belt, then he sat at the kitchen island and waited until she emerged from the bedroom. She still had a haunted, tired, appearance about her though.

"Let's grab something to eat on the way."

"*Sure.*" She pulled on one of her stylish jackets, and they were on their way out the door.

Jaden allowed him to drive and sat in the backseat, unusual behavior for her. He glanced in the rearview mirror at his partner. She seemed quieter than usual as they made their way through mid-morning traffic toward the station, only speaking once to indicate her preference for tea when they went through the drive-through on the way to the office. He drove her SUV into their assigned unit spot underneath headquarters. He got out of the car, carrying his coffee, and headed inside before he realized Jaden hadn't followed him.

Going around the SUV, he opened the rear door and found her curled up in the backseat, asleep. Damn. He pulled the emergency blanket out, tucked it around her, and locked the doors. Jaden would be safe there while he made a quick stop at the office.

Cameron made his way to the seventh floor, through multiple elevators and security. The board on the wall declared the floor dedicated to Homicide, but that wasn't completely true. Tucked into a corner room, which he swore was a converted broom closet, Special Investigations went almost unnoticed by most officers and members of the public.

"Whoa, Olsen." Detective Bill Wilson stuck his foot out to stop him. "What's the rush?"

"In the middle of a case." He had to stop himself from sighing at the guy's petty jealousy over not getting the post with Jaden.

"Yeah, where's your mind reader, anyway? She didn't turn up dead this morning, did she?" Bill's words and callous tone set his protective instincts into overdrive.

"What the hell does that mean?" he snapped.

"You didn't see the case summaries from yesterday?" Bill narrowed his eyes as Cam shook his head. "Chick that could be Detective Black's sister showed up dead. Floater in the river."

"Really?" Icy tendrils shot down his spine. "How long was she in the water?"

"Week, week and a half. Third one this summer we've found." He shook his head. "Only saw photos of her, had to ID the floater with dental records. The others were strangled, and damn if they both don't look a lot like Black. The floater though, fuck...."

"I'm sure it's just a crazy coincidence."

"That or your mind reader has a secret admirer."

"Fuck off." He pushed past Bill and the others, stalking into the tiny room serving as their office, trying to brush off the heebie-jeebies from Bill's words.

In one corner sat a comfortable armchair for Jaden when she needed a break. Mounds of files and three small desks occupied the rest of the space in their broom closet office.

Ruth glanced over from her desk as he came in. "Hi, honey. Where's Jaden?"

He shut the door so they wouldn't be disturbed. "In the parking garage, asleep in the backseat of the SUV."

Ruth frowned "Really? That's not good."

"I know." He walked to his desk. "She's starting to worry me. She saw one of the missing girls get murdered yesterday." Ruth knew the full extent of Jaden's power, maybe even more so than he did.

"Fuck me in the ass. No wonder you haven't been in the office."

"It's not a great place when her walls are down."

Ruth made a noise of acknowledgment. Her phone rang. "Special Investigations. This is Ruth." It must be someone important for her to answer the phone properly. "Yes, sir. Yes, Judge Silva. I'll send him over right away. Yes, sir, thank you, sir." She dropped the receiver back in the cradle. "Judge Silva says if you bring him the warrant, he'll sign it in between cases." She handed him the typed warrant, ready to go except for the signature. "You've got about thirty to get over to the courthouse."

"Damn." That would be tight, but he could do it. "Thanks, Ruth. I'll call you as soon as I have it, then get on the horn to Paige Clark over at CPS. Tell her I'm on my way with the warrant, so she should get the Jenkins's files in order. I can't afford to wait around all day for her."

"No problem, boss."

Hurrying out of his office and through the cubical farm to the elevators, he avoided the on-call area when he headed downstairs. He'd had enough of Wilson's bullshit for one day.

Jaden was still asleep when he returned to the SUV—not that he had been gone long. Pulling out of the garage, he hit the streets, speeding a bit, and used his lights and sirens once or twice to get through a red light. He made it to the courthouse with ten minutes to spare. After parking in the secure parking area, he flagged over a patrol officer who leaned on the hood of his cruiser, drinking coffee.

Cam flashed his badge. "Detective Olsen. You busy?"

The patrol officer, whose nametag read "McKenzie",

shrugged. "Waiting for my partner in court. Could be a while."

Cam tossed him the keys to the SUV. "Make sure no one messes with the SUV," he instructed. "My partner is in the back, she's pretty sick, you know how it is."

McKenzie nodded. "Yeah, I got it. Keep your sick days for when you're dead. I'll watch her for ya. No problem."

"Thanks, shouldn't be more than twenty minutes." He jogged into the courthouse, clutching the folder with the warrant.

He made it to the judge's chambers and didn't even have a chance to tell the law clerk he was waiting for Judge Silva when the judge came barreling in, his long black robes billowing behind him. "Olsen," he said. "Excellent, I have a lunch date, and I don't want this to take too much of my time. Come." He motioned for Cameron to follow him into the inner chambers. The Judge removed his robes and sat behind his desk.

Cam handed him the folder. "I need a warrant signed for the records of a foster home run by Donald and Vanessa Jenkins. Three girls, missing and presumed dead, were in their care over the last four years or so. All three of the girls reported abuse happening while they were living there." He took a breath. "The Jenkins's home was a transitional foster home. Some kids may have only spent a night there. I need to look at their files and cross-reference everyone who's gone through there with our missing person's' files to see if anyone else pops up. We also need to see if three other missing girls linked to the first three I mentioned went through there or had contact with the Jenkinses during that timeframe."

The Judge read through the files and regarded him. "Sounds like a bit of a fishing expedition to me."

"I know, Your Honor. It's tough to release such a large number of records to me with so little to go on. Usually, I would only ask for the records of the missing girls, but because the Jenkinses were a transitional foster home, mentions of the missing girls being there might not have made it into their files, especially if it was a short period of time. Some kids went through their care literally in the space of a day. I just need to cover all of my bases, Judge. I need to make sure there are no more missing girls I can link to the Jenkinses."

Silva stroked his short silver beard. "Here's the deal. I'll write the warrant to release names and birth dates of the children. Not their full files. You get the full files for all of the missing girls, and, if your fishing expedition turns up any more names, come back and I'll amend the warrant to add them in as well."

"Thank you, sir. That sounds very fair."

Silva nodded, and proceeded to write the changes into the warrant and sign it. Rising, he handed it to him. "Here you go, son. I hope you find what you need."

"Thank you, Your Honor." He took the warrant and shook the judge's hand before leaving his chambers and hurrying to the SUV.

McKenzie leaned on the hood of his cruiser. He played with his phone, appearing bored, but the fact he looked up as soon as Cam walked outside told him he had been paying close attention. He had to be younger than Cameron, maybe in his mid-twenties, but he had been around for a few years, judging by his demeanor.

"Hey, Detective Olsen," he said, sliding the phone into the case hanging off his vest as he approached.

"Everything all right?"

"Yup. Didn't hear anything from her, and no one messed with the car."

"Thanks. Which precinct are you out of?"

McKenzie handed him the keys to the SUV. "Third precinct, rotation two," he said, with a bright-white smile. His gray eyes sparkled.

"Who's your sarge?"

"Sergeant O'Neil."

"Excellent. Thanks for your help, constable."

Jaden stayed asleep as he pulled out of the lot and into the midday traffic. He called Ruth to tell her to give Paige a warning—he would be arriving shortly, search warrant in hand.

Chapter Six

On their way to the Jenkins's place, Jaden woke and ate the cold bagel left in the car from that morning. He detoured through the nearest drive-though, getting them hot coffees on their way out of town. Allowing the GPS to guide him around in the unfamiliar neighborhood, he turned right, past the sign for the subdivision.

"*Are you sure you can do this?*" he asked her.

"*Yes. I'll be fine. As long as I don't punch the bastard's lights out the second I see him.*"

He laughed. Tiny Jaden punching anyone out seem absurd. She may be a police detective, but she barely passed the physical requirements.

The GPS told him to turn left onto a side street then arrive at his destination. He slowed down, searching for number twenty-one. Despite the "No Parking" signs, he pulled the SUV in front of the house. The neighborhood appeared older than most subdivisions, big oak trees and large lots with well-proportioned houses seeming the norm with the occasional new boxy build for good measure.

A van sat in the driveway, and the main door to the house stood open as they approached the front—someone had to be home. He rang the doorbell.

A woman in her late forties appeared from somewhere out of sight and stalked toward the door. "Whatever you're selling, or whatever religion you represent, I'm not interested. Can't you read?" She pointed to the "No Soliciting" sign stuck next to the door.

"Vanessa Jenkins?"

She couldn't hide her surprise that they knew her name. "Yes."

"Ma'am, I'm Detective Olsen." Cameron flashed his badge. "This is Detective Black of the Special Investigations Unit with the Toronto PD. May we come in?"

"What's this about?" She didn't move to open the door.

"*Ma'am.*" Jaden moved her lips so Vanessa wouldn't clue into the fact she used her mind to speak, which sounded just like someone talking, and not her vocal chords. "*We're investigating several missing children. We know you were a foster family for some of them, and we were hoping you could tell us what you remember about each child.*"

"All right." She unlocked the screen door and opened it to them. "I don't know if I can be of much help. Most of the kids were only here a short time."

"We know that, ma'am. Anything you can help with is greatly appreciated."

"Sure. I need to go bring my mother-in-law out to the garden. We can talk out there," she said, leading them into the house. She showed them to the french doors leading outside. "I'll be right back, please make yourself at home."

Cameron went to offer to help, just so he could keep an eye on her, but a glance from Jaden stopped him. "Thank you, ma'am."

When she disappeared around the corner, Jaden turned to him. "*Donald's mother had a stroke about a year ago, she's been living with them ever since. Vanessa couldn't take care of her and foster children at the same time so they gave up fostering. I think she is bitter about it.*"

He nodded. "*Is she really going to get her mother in-law?*"

"*Yes, we interrupted her from getting her to the bathroom*

and changed."

Vanessa Jenkins must have been a very easy read for Jaden to get all of that in the brief contact they had with her so far.

Vanessa returned a few minutes later, pushing an older lady in a wheelchair. "Over there. I want to soak up the sun."

"Yes, Mom."

"Who are these people? They had better not be trying to sell me no new-fangled religion! I got my own, thanks. I'm a good Catholic girl, I'll have you know."

"No, Mom. They're police officers. They want my help on an investigation. Sit here and enjoy your sunshine." Frustration filled her voice. "I'll be right over there."

She walked to where they sat, politely remaining quiet. "Sorry about that. Can I get you anything? Tea, coffee...juice?"

"We're fine, thank you. Have a seat."

Vanessa sat, regarding them with mild curiosity. He pulled out the first photo of Taylor. "Can you tell me what you remember about her?" He handed her the photo. "Her name is Taylor Kalinin. She would have come through here about three or so years ago."

Vanessa squinted at the photo. Then her eyes grew wide. "Yes, I remember her. She was a handful. She didn't stay very long, less than a month. Kept making up crazy stories."

Jaden's eyes narrowed in response, her tell for someone not being truthful with them. *"What kind of stories?"*

"Oh, you know, the usual. Her mom was a crack head and a prostitute. She wasn't above selling her daughter for some extra money. She was a mess by the time we got her, always saying how her mom was coming back to get her when she found a rich boyfriend. She told her CPS worker her teacher tried to touch her and my husband was trying to sleep with her. She thought any man showing the slightest bit of affection toward her was trying to abuse her, poor kid." She shook her head and handed the photo to him.

"She believes most of that. She's not totally convinced everything Taylor said was made up, though."

"All right, what about this girl?" He handed her Olivia's photo.

"Oh, Liv, we had her for a long time, and her older sister Avery for a short while. Avery got placed right away; she was a smart kid and had good grades, despite raising her little sister. Liv was pretty broken though. Think something wasn't quite right with her, she didn't know how to function without her sister. I wanted to keep both of them, but we were just a transitional house, they wouldn't let us," Vanessa explained.

"Do you know Avery's current location?" he asked. Maybe they could pay a visit to Olivia's sister.

"No, sorry, I lost touch with her after she was adopted."

"What else do you remember about Olivia?"

Vanessa shrugged. "Not much, sorry. I saw so many kids over the years they all start to blur together."

"Liar, she remembers more, but is holding back," she shot over to him. He gave her an almost imperceptible nod.

Cameron took the photo and handed her the last photo of Emily. "What about her?"

Vanessa smiled sadly. "Emily Knight. I remember her really well. She was the last kid we took before"—she shot a nasty glance over at her mother-in-law—"before Mom got sick and I couldn't do it anymore."

"What do you remember about her?"

"She wasn't like most kids that came through here. She was from a good home. Two parents, stable. Tragic really, how she got here. Her parents killed in a car accident. Then it took them months and months to decide her grandmother was unfit. I met the woman several times. She might have been older, but she loved Emily more than anything and it showed. Emily would have been better off with her." Vanessa sighed. "She kept running back to her grandmother's, not that I blame her. I always thought it would have been better if they took her away right away, rather than letting it drag on so long."

He nodded sympathetically. "Did anything happen while Emily was here?"

Vanessa looked from him to Jaden and back again. "Sort of." She hesitated. They both remained silent, forcing her to talk. "Emily wasn't used to this environment. She didn't know the rule about always knocking on the door and waiting for an answer before you enter. She walked in on my husband in the bathroom once. It was innocent, but she got freaked out, then told her grandmother what happened. They filed a report. CPS said it was unfounded."

"*Oh, she is sooo lying. Call her on it.*"

He shushed his partner. He showed Vanessa photos of the other three girls, not surprisingly she had never seen or heard of any of them before, except Marissa, whose photo and story have been in the news. The search of their records didn't turn up any more missing kids, particularly blonde girls, who could be linked to the case, and the other three girls were never in their care.

"Vanessa," her mother-in-law shouted. "Get me an iced tea."

"In a minute, Mom. I need to show the detectives out first."

"I'm going to die of dehydration if I don't get one right now," she spoke with a pronounced slur.

"Sorry, I'll be right back." Vanessa disappeared into the house.

The mother-in-law turned and grinned at both of them, beckoning Jaden forward. "*Is everything alright, Mrs. Jenkins?*" Jaden projected her thoughts so he could hear their conversation as well.

"Now you listen here, little one." She eyed Jaden. "Vanessa might not want to admit what her husband is, but I know my own son."

"*You know what, Mrs. Jenkins?*"

"My son abused those girls." Her voice had no trace of hesitation or the slurring he had noticed earlier. "I can't prove it, but I can see it as sure as I can see my nose." She pointed to her out-of-joint, pointy nose. "He's always had a taste for the little ones. Damn government was giving him an unlimited supply until I moved in. Had to find a way to stop it." She nodded. "You go ahead and do some digging, sweetie." She patted Jaden's arm.

"You'll find the proof."

"*Thank you, Mrs. Jenkins.*" She moved away just as Vanessa returned with a glass of iced tea.

"Here you go, Mom."

Mrs. Jenkins eyed the glass. "Why did you get me that? I hate iced tea. I said I wanted water," she growled, her slur returning.

Cameron had to bite his lip to control his laughter.

Vanessa sighed. "All right, let me show the detectives out, and I'll bring you water, okay?"

"Fine, but be quick about it," Mrs. Jenkins snapped.

Vanessa led them to the door. "Sorry about her. She keeps getting more and more confused each day."

"*It's all right,*" Jaden assured her. "*We got everything we needed today. Sorry to take up so much of your time.*"

"I'm sorry I couldn't be of more help." Vanessa ushered them out then shut and locked both doors behind them. Well, if that wasn't a sign.

As soon as they were out of ear shot, Jaden cackled. "*What a great old lady.*" She held her hand out for the keys; he handed them over. She climbed behind the wheel of her SUV.

"*What did you get from her?*" He climbed in the passenger seat and buckled his seatbelt. Jaden took off as soon as his door shut.

"*That her son, Donald, has been raping little girls since he was a teenager. What a bastard. He has a nice collection of kiddie porn hidden in the basement and in his office, which we can use as an in to start an investigation by the Special Crimes unit.*" She flew through the subdivision—ignoring the GPS, which screamed at her to make a U-turn to go to the office. "*She's convinced he only goes for girls that are easy for him. She doesn't see him hurting Marissa or the others, also he was home yesterday when Emily was murdered.*"

"*You know this means we're out of connections besides Meincke right?*"

Jaden nodded. "*I know, at least we can kill two birds with one stone with the Jenkins case.*"

"*Shut down a rapist and get an in with the unit,*" he replied.

"*Pretty much. Think we can get a search warrant for the house? His mother knew where the hiding spots are. They're not that hard to find.*" She roared out onto the main artery, and when someone blew his horn at her, she flashed her reds and blues at him. She continued on her way unimpeded into the express lanes, apart from the occasional horn or dirty glare from fellow drivers as she cut them off.

"*Glad to know you're feeling better.*"

"*What?*" She smiled at him, batting her long lashes at him "*Get Ruth going on the search warrant for the Jenkins's house and amend the other search warrant to find Avery Simon's records—I want to talk to her. In the meantime, let's go talk to Emily's grandmother. She might be able to give us something more on Emily.*"

"*Sure, sounds good.*" He made the phone calls while Jaden drove them to the retirement residence where, according to Emily's paper work, Evelyn Knight lived.

They parked in front and went in. The lady at the front desk ignored them, focused on filing her nails. After long moments, she dragged her attention away from her nails. "What do you want?"

He flashed his badge. "Detective Olsen, this is Detective Black, we're looking for Evelyn Knight," he said.

"Oh, um, hang on a second, I'll get the manager." She picked up the phone and dialed a number. "Can you come to the front desk?" she asked the person on the other end of the line. "There are police here about Mrs. Knight." She paused then disconnected. "The manager will be here shortly."

Less than a minute later, a woman in her mid-forties with shoulder-length blonde hair in a severe business suit appeared from one of the hallways. "Hello, I'm Jennifer Martin, General Manager for the Royal Place Retirement Residence." She approached them, exchanging glances with the girl working the front desk.

"*She's nervous about something.*"

He shot Jaden a quick stare. He could have figured that out without a telepath, thank you.

"Detective Olsen, this is Detective Black, with the Special Investigations Unit of the Toronto Police Department. I would like to speak to Evelyn Knight."

"Why don't we step into my office?" She motioned for them to follow her down the hallway.

"What's up, Jay?"

"Let her explain." That meant she knew exactly what was going on but wasn't able to explain in the time provided.

"Please sit down." Jennifer showed them into a neat office. They took the two comfortable chairs across the desk from her. She sat down and folded her hands on her desk. "I'm very sorry to inform you Mrs. Knight passed away this morning."

His heart dropped. *Damn.* "What happened?"

"It appears as though Mrs. Knight had a heart attack last night in her sleep. I'm very sorry."

"That's very sad to hear. We were coming here today to talk to her about her missing granddaughter, Emily."

"Of course, Mrs. Knight was heartbroken Emily ran away like that. She was never the same afterward." Jennifer shook her head.

"Do you know if there is any family remaining, or maybe friends who we could talk to?"

"She has someone listed as next of kin here. They live out in Vancouver, but I'm not sure how much help they would be." She flipped through files on her desk. "There are two ladies she was friends with here. They're handling her arrangements for her." She pulled out a sheet of paper and handed it to them. "This is the information for her next of kin. We've already called her to inform her of Mrs. Knight's passing."

"What about her friends?" he asked.

"They'll probably be in the lounge. If you'd like to follow me, I can take you there and introduce you to them."

"Why don't you take Detective Black to meet them? Would you mind if I borrowed your office for a moment to call Mrs.

Knight's next of kin?" He pulled out his cell phone.

"Go ahead. Take all the time you need." Jennifer stood and showed Jaden toward the door. "Please follow me this way, Detective Black."

Chapter Seven

"Do you want the good news or the bad news?" Ruth asked as they walked into their office an hour or so later.

Cameron sighed, "Bad news first."

"No dice on a warrant for Jenkins's homes. Not without a current complainant."

"Good news?"

"We got the amended warrant for Avery Simon, now Avery Mercier. Olivas's older sister. She goes to a private school a block and a half away. If you hurry, you'll be able to pull her just as her last class of the day starts." Ruth handed them the file on Avery.

"Thanks, Ruth, you're the best." He took the file and hurried out of the office, along with Jaden. He glanced through the file in the elevator. Officially adopted three years ago at the age of thirteen, extremely rare. Been in foster care since she was the age of eight, had been placed with the adoptive family since she was ten. They refused to take her sister Olivia, though. Avery was sixteen and a senior in high school. He glanced at her test scores. Kid had to be a genius.

He handed the file to Jaden as they made their way out the front. It seemed pointless to drive, as the school was a block and a half away. They made their way through mid-day downtown Toronto, dodging taxis, construction, and other pedestrians.

As they climbed the front steps of the school, security personnel in jackets bearing the school crest stopped them.

"Detectives Olsen and Black, Toronto PD." Cameron flashed his badge. "We need to speak to one of your students about an ongoing investigation."

The security guard used his radio. "Go on into the office. Principal Thomas will see you. Through the main doors, the office is your first door on the right."

"Thank you." He held the door open for Jaden. She walked in ahead of him. The archway into the school stated it had been built in the 1920s, and it smelled of chalk and old gym lockers and strongly reminded him of his old high school back east. They entered the office, and the secretary glanced at them.

"Principal Thomas will be out in a moment," she said, before returning to her computer.

A tall, slim man, with black hair and a graying moustache and wearing a navy suit walked out of the inner office a few moments later. "I'm Principal Jim Thomas. How can I be of assistance to you?"

"I'm Detective Olsen and this is Detective Black. We're from the Special Investigations Unit with the Toronto Police Department. We'd like to speak to one of your students, Avery Mercier, regarding an investigation."

"Avery is one of our best students, is she in some kind of trouble?" His concern seemed genuine.

"Not at all. We would like to ask for her help in an ongoing investigation."

"I'll go pull her from class. You can use the spare office."

"Thank you very much, Principal Thomas."

The secretary showed them into the spare office and they waited for Avery. She appeared five minutes later.

She wasn't what Cameron expected. She had short, spiky black hair with purple highlights. The nose piercing and lip ring did little to distract from the heavy black make-up, like a slightly younger, anger-filled Jaden. "Thomas said you wanted to see me." She threw herself into the chair opposite them and glared at

Jaden. "You don't look like a cop."

"*You don't look like a senior in high school.*" Answer attitude with attitude.

"What do you want? You're not supposed to talk to a minor without a parent present. My dad's a lawyer, he'll have both your badges."

Jaden opened Olivia's folder and slid the photo of her sister across the desk to her. "*We're here about Olivia.*"

Avery's demeanor changed in an instant. She deflated. "Did you find her?" she all but whispered.

"*No, not yet. We're investigating her disappearance along with several other girls the same age and description. We were hoping you could help us.*"

Avery chewed her lower lip and blinked away tears. "Anything."

"*Olivia disappeared in June of 2009, correct?*"

"Yeah, it was just after her birthday. My parents had her over for a birthday dinner. I wanted them to adopt her like they adopted me." Tears leaked out of the corner of her eyes, and Jaden handed her some Kleenex. She sniffled. "Olivia isn't smart like me. My biological mom was using while she was pregnant with Liv. She always had problems ever since she was a baby. My parents couldn't handle her full-time. I tried to tell them it wouldn't be a problem, I would look after her and everything, but...." She shrugged.

"*You took care of her?*"

"I had to. Made it look really nice when Child Services came around so they wouldn't take her away. Didn't help."

"*You did everything you could for your sister. Do you remember some of the foster homes you were in together?*"

Avery shook her head but then nodded. "Maybe. There weren't many. Not many people wanted an eight-year-old and a one-year-old." She thought some more. "The first place they took us, Ms. Clare, she was nice. Let me keep taking care of Liv. We were only there a few weeks then we went to the Jenkins's place." Avery shivered.

"We know Olivia filed a report detailing she was abused at the Jenkins's." She tried to offer a way for Avery to trust to her. *"We thought you might know something about it."*

"I guess." She crossed her arms over her chest. Her chin had a defiant tilt to it. She started to shut down just when they needed her to open up the most.

"I know it's tough to talk about, but we really need to know what happened."

Avery stared down at the desk. "Stuff, lots of bad stuff. I filed the report for Liv. I'm okay, you know, strong enough. I mean she was just a baby when we got there. They placed me pretty quick, but it took them ages to find her a permanent foster home. I couldn't stand the thought of him hurting Liv. I mean she wasn't even three when he hurt her! How can someone do that? The CPS said it was unfounded. How could they do that?" Avery shook her head. Tears tracked down her face, smudging her makeup.

"Avery," Cameron said in his softest, most gentle voice. "Did Mr. Jenkins touch you as well as your sister?"

Avery dabbed angrily at the tears trailing down her face. She nodded.

"Did he take any photographs of you?" he asked.

She nodded again, more tears pouring down her face.

"Oh, sweetie." Jaden stood and went over to her. She knelt down in front of where Avery sat. *"It will be okay."* She opened her arms and held Avery as she cried.

∞

Cameron pulled the bulletproof vest on over his shirt, his suit jacket tossed into the backseat of the SUV. He listened to the com system as the specialized entry team prepared to hit the Jenkins's place. He stood next to their mobile command post, several blocks away, watching the video screen from the camera mounted on one of the officers.

They breached the front door, screaming, "Search warrant." It didn't take long for them to arrest Donald Jenkins and detain

Vanessa and her mother-in-law.

Cameron drove them from the mobile command unit over to the house. As they arrived, the entry team escorted Jenkins out to the waiting patrol car. They would have him under arrest for Avery's abuse, and anything else they would uncover in the home. The wife and the mother were being held in the living room while they searched for illegal pornography. Cameron entered, followed by Jaden. They went straight to the basement and found the first box of photographs hidden in the rafters, where his mother-in-law had believed it to be.

They each snapped on a pair of gloves before pulling the box down, going through the pictures. They made him sick, but it was enough to call in the child Sex Crimes Unit without having to bullshit a reason. They would be able to kill two birds with one stone. Get Jenkins in jail and find out what happened to Marissa and the other missing girls.

He dialed Ruth and asked her to patch him through to the on-call detective. He tapped his foot, annoyed by the hold music. At last, someone answered.

"Detective Leann Steele, Special Crimes Unit."

"Hi, Detective Steele, it's Detective Olsen with the Special Investigations Unit. How are you doing?"

"Fine, thank you. What can I help you with, Detective Olsen?"

"Please, call me Cameron." He laid on the charm. "In the course of one of our investigations we raided a former foster home. We found several boxes of child pornography. Some of it appears homemade. I was wondering if someone in your unit would be able to come over and check it out."

"Sure, I'm on call along with Detective Meincke. I'd be happy to give Special Investigations a hand. Give me the address, and we'll head over there immediately."

He gave her the address and disconnected. While he was on the phone, Jaden uncovered two more boxes of photos, one of videos, and several photo albums. "Christ, looks like some of the stuff goes back to the early nineties," he commented, as she flipped through an album.

It had photographs next to notes on how good they were. Rating five-and-six-year-olds on how good they were sexually— that was just sick.

"It's very sick. Did she give you an ETA?"

"No, but they're at the office, so at least thirty minutes, maybe longer. Shorter if they use lights. Do you think you got all of the boxes?"

"Yeah, but it will be worth having CSU sweep it again, just in case I missed any."

"Let's go check out the office." They carried the boxes upstairs and handed them to the Crime Scene Unit techs who had arrived to process the home. CSU bagged and tagged them while they went to search the office.

Jaden found a laptop hidden in the desk. Password locked, but he had no doubt the computer guys over at the station would be able to crack the code and get onto it. He suspected it contained more illicit images, and maybe even video.

They were going through another album that had been hidden in plain sight on the bookshelf when a patrol officer walked in. "Sorry to bother you, Detectives, but two detectives from the Special Crimes Unit are here asking to see you."

"Show them in, thanks," Cameron replied.

In walked a stocky redhead, her long hair pulled into a ponytail, wearing an ill-fitting man's suit, and a thin man with a moustache and a receding hair line in a polyester number that seemed to be of an identical make and model to his partner's; wrong size. "Detective Leann Steele," the redhead said, holding out her hand.

Cameron held up his gloved hand. "Detective Olsen, please call me Cameron. This is Detective Jaden Black."

"Oh, sorry. Gloves, right? Nice to meet both of you. What do we have?" Steele asked as she walked over to them.

"Several boxes of photos and videos CSU techs are processing, as well as numerous photo albums. They seem to be arranged according to age and sex. There are photos and notes...rating them."

"*Steele seems a bit disgusted by the rating thing but is trying to remain professional. Meincke is hard to get a read on. Like he's hiding something.*"

"Let's see." Meincke strolled over to the book. He went to touch it with his bare hands and Jaden stopped him, shoving a pair of gloves at him. "Oh, sorry," he apologized.

"*He's far too excited to see kiddie porn.*"

Cameron had to stop himself from rolling his eyes; he always got a laugh when his telepathic partner pointed out the obvious.

"We think he's been doing this since the early nineties, if not before. A lot of it appears homemade, but some might be stuff off the Internet at well. We seized a laptop the techs will have to have a crack at it."

"Excellent. Thank you for all of your help, we'll take it from here," Meincke said, not diverting his gaze from the album.

"*Tell him no.*"

"Sorry, but I called you in as a consult on this investigation." He removed the album from Meincke's hands with a little more force than necessary. "I'm running the show, and if you have any problem with that, you can take it up with Chief Novak."

"Unlike you, I don't have a direct line to the Chief of Police's office."

"Boys," Leann interrupted, "there is more than enough stuff here to keep all of us busy for the next week. Stop fighting. Since Cameron called us in, Special Investigations is lead on this."

Meincke shot Leann an evil glare, then replied, "Sorry, Leann is right, you're lead."

"Thank you." Cam reexamined the album. Mostly girls around the age of eight and nine. He flipped through until he came to the picture of Avery. "Bingo."

He showed Jaden the photo, who nodded.

"Is that your complainant?" Leann asked.

"Yeah, we tracked down some former foster kids, and this one pointed us here. We didn't call you in until we knew for sure what we were dealing with."

"She looks familiar," Meincke said, staring at the photo of

Avery. "I'm sure we've spoken to her before."

"She said she never filed any report. This was over seven years ago." His heart pounded in his ears. If Meincke made the connection to Olivia, their cover could be blown. Assuming he was responsible for the missing girls, of course.

Meincke shook his head. "Never mind, must be another girl that looks like her."

Leann flicked through her phone. "We've had a couple of complaints against Mr. Jenkins in the past. CPS said they were all unfounded."

Jaden shook her head but didn't speak. He knew she didn't want to give away her secret to them. Her mind speak was very powerful, but if she was having a rough day, then she could mess up her lip synching, and that was the last thing they wanted. They didn't want Meincke or Steele to know about her talents.

"CPS dropped the ball on this one," he supplied for Jaden. He knew his partner well enough to know what she would be thinking in this situation.

"Pretty much," Leann replied.

Meincke flipped through the album and had his cell phone out.

"*He's snapping photos of the photos.*"

Cameron startled, he hadn't expected his partner to speak at that moment.

"*He's trying to make it look like he's researching information on the girls. How could Leann not notice? He's so blatant. Fuck, Cam, I think he might be our guy.*"

"*Fuck me in the ass,*" he replied, using Ruth's catch phrase. "*I'll stop him.*" He went to the desk, where Meincke had separated himself from the rest of them. "Find anything on the girls?"

Meincke jumped a tiny bit. "Not yet. We should take this to the office. I'll have better luck accessing older files."

"CSU is going to process everything first. I want every page checked for fingerprints or DNA. There is no way he's going to pull the whole 'it was planted' routine. I want dead proof Jenkins knew about the photographs and videos."

"Of course. How long before we can go through them?" Meincke asked, anxiously.

"Tomorrow morning at the earliest," he replied. "Jenkins lawyered up and is refusing to talk."

"Great, a perp with a lawyer." Leann sighed. "Why don't we start fresh at the office tomorrow, then?" she suggested, interrupting them. "We can comb through this, see if we have any matching files, plus we can see what the techs can get off of the computer."

"I think that's an excellent idea," he told Leann.

"Matt, go and get the CSU techs," she instructed. He wanted to argue, Cameron could see it on his face, but he turned on his heel and disappeared out of the office. "Look, I know Matt's a bit hard to get along with at first, but he's a really good detective. Just give him a chance."

"I'll keep that in mind," he said.

Meincke returned with a CSU tech. After some brief instructions from Cameron, they left the CSU techs to it.

Leann and Meincke took off in their car while Jaden drove her SUV and he rode shotgun. Rush hour had finished over an hour ago, and the expressway had more or less emptied out. It didn't take long for his partner to pull into the underground parking garage of her building, after a brief stop at his place so he could grab enough clothing for the next few days.

Both were so exhausted Jaden caved and ordered food in from her favorite Greek dive around the corner.

They scarfed down their food and in silence before Jaden hurried to her laptop. She focused on that, shutting him out for the time being. He didn't take offence to her ignoring him; he could see she needed some space.

He borrowed Jaden's desktop and checked his personal e-mail. Jaden announced she wanted to go to bed at just after nine. He said goodnight and finished an e-mail to his mom and another one to his little sister before following her to bed.

He found Jaden already asleep on her side with David tucked

in next to her. She had slept most of the morning, and he hadn't expected to see her asleep already. Leaning down, he planted a kiss on her forehead before getting ready for bed and sliding in next to her. He listened to her even breathing, letting it lull him to sleep.

Chapter Eight

The black dragon didn't startle him as he would have expected. Instead, he trusted her.

"Come." She held out her wing. "Sleep." She scooped him up, cradling him with her wing, giving him the sensation he rested in a hammock. He felt safe and warm, and it lulled him to sleep.

He jolted awake and found himself lying in a hammock, staring at trees growing by his cabin on the lake in the Muskokas. He was there, at his cabin, but there were no sounds of wildlife or smell of the woods. The place was familiar but somehow wrong at the same time.

"Hello, Cameron."

He jumped and turned. A tall blond man stood next to the hammock. "Do I know you?" He recognized him, from something on the edge of his consciousness.

"Oh sorry, here, allow me." The man waved his hand, and all the memories swirled back him, dragons, the Dreamworld, and the hotel. His cheeks heated as he remembered what had happened with Jaden. Did they really make love?

His head hurt—overwhelmed with everything he had to take in. "How did you do that?"

"I'm a dream master," Paul said.

Cameron knew his name; he remembered it from the night

before.

Paul dropped himself into the hammock next to him. "In this world, I can do anything I want."

"How did I end up here?"

"You felt like you were in a hammock, and your brain connected the memory of a hammock with your cabin. The more you thought about your cabin the more it became your cabin. The Dreamworld is about wishes and wants. It's not black and white like the waking world."

"Is that why...?" He paused at the thought of what he had done with Jaden the previous night while in Dreamworld.

"Yes. Don't worry. I'm not mad. I figured it would happen. Jaden's been in love with you for a long time."

The hammock rocked with their weight. He felt a bit stunned. She was in love with him? Other than sleeping with him in last night's dream, she had given no outward signs. "How do you know this?"

The older man shrugged. "I've known Jaden longer than she's known herself."

"What does that mean?"

"Everything and nothing all at the same time."

He sighed in frustration. Paul's words didn't make any sense. "Do you always talk in riddles?"

"Not always."

He sighed again. "Then just explain."

"Are you sure you want to know?" Paul turned to him, his eyes twinkling with mischief.

"Yes."

"Alright, I'll explain, but you're not going to like it." The other man swung the hammock with his foot, staring at the perfect blue sky with the occasional puffy white cloud floating by. Paul's side pressed against his, and he couldn't deny the unmistakable pull he felt toward the other man.

"I was born a twin. My sister's name was Adeline. Our mother died in childbirth," he stated. "My mother was a telepath. Most psychic abilities like ours run in families. Usually the oldest child gets the ability when the parents pass on. Sometimes it skips to another child, sometimes it skips to another generation, and sometimes the ability is divided between two children."

"You and your twin sister?"

"Usually your parent spends time training you to receive the abilities. My mother was very powerful. She could read the minds of people in the waking world and in the sleeping world. When she died, I got her abilities in the sleeping world, and Adeline got the abilities for the waking world."

"As babies?"

"Yes. Our aunt raised us. We were two parts of a whole. We did everything together, but it was too much for Adeline. She never learned to control her gifts, so she turned to things to make them go away instead." He stared off into the distance.

"Drugs?"

"And drinking," he acknowledged. "She OD'd when we were eighteen."

"How does Jaden come into the picture?"

"Jaden is, for lack of a better word, a reincarnation of Adeline."

"You're kidding, right?"

"Nope. You know what Jaden appears like here?"

He thought of the long flowing hair and the curves and the laugh lines around her eyes. "Yes."

"It's what Adeline looked like. What she might have look like today. Jaden, for all intents and purposes, is Adeline. Except, she is far more powerful than Adeline ever was. I spent years searching for my Adeline after she died. My aunt said she would reincarnate as someone new, as she had no children and no other family member inherited her abilities. I found Jaden in Dreamworld when she was just three. I taught her here how to be out there. I guided her and helped her. I stopped her from making the same mistakes Adeline did." Paul glanced away. "I brought her to you."

"To me?"

Paul nodded.

"How? Why?"

"Because you're her mate. For each telepath there is one true mate in the entire world. Their mate is the sole person who can block their abilities without harm, enhance them, even make them more powerful in some cases. Not all telepaths find their mate, for whatever reason. My mother never found hers."

The news stunned him. "I don't understand. I'm, like, twelve years older than Jaden. How am I her mate?"

"Because you were Adeline's mate," Paul whispered. "I knew the moment Jaden met you. It's like...pure energy radiating from you into her. I can't even describe it."

His head hurt. "I never met Adeline, I knew nothing about her. How was I her mate?"

The older man shook his head. He stared at the blue sky, as though trying to hide the pain radiating from him. "You never met Adeline because she died before you were supposed to meet. Fate can be cruel like that sometimes."

"Wait. If I'm supposed to be Jaden's mate and Jaden is Adeline, and you and Adeline are twins and share everything, does that mean I'm supposed to be your mate as well?" he asked, his brain starting to make sense of everything Paul had told him.

"Like I said, fate is cruel."

"Why do you say that?"

"Because only one of us can be happy. I mean truly happy. We can't both have you."

Cameron lay in the hammock, quiet for a long time, his brain swirling. All of the sudden, things in his life made so much sense. He had always been attracted to men and women equally, having his fair share of both over the years. He had decided, in his early twenties, he would fuck men and have relationships with women. Neither worked out how he had hoped. "Why not? Why can't you both have me?"

The other man stared at him, shocked. "It wouldn't be right."

"Who says what's right and what's wrong?" he challenged.

Paul stared up at the sky again. "How would it be fair to you? To Jaden, to me, both of us wanting your attention, often at the same time?"

Cameron moved in the hammock, wishing they laid on something more solid. He moved closer to the smaller man, his hand touching his side. "I always thought there was something wrong with me. I was never happy in a relationship solely with women, and men just left me wanting more. What if you're right, that I'm supposed to be a mate to both of you?"

Paul groaned, very low. Cameron found himself in his condo, in his room, lying in bed next to Paul rather than in the hammock. "There is one way to find out," Paul whispered.

"Am I going to remember this in the morning?" Cameron rolled onto his side, propping himself on his elbow, his hand resting on his new lover's stomach.

"Do you want to?" Paul reached out to touch his five o'clock shadow, his fingers scratching over the rough whiskers.

He thought about it. Did he want to forget everything about Paul? About Jaden? He didn't want to wake up wondering what had just happened and feeling like he missed a big part of something. "Yes, I want to remember everything."

The older man tilted his chin, and Cameron brought his head downward until their lips met. He kissed, soft, hesitant at first. They explored, finding small ways to make each other moan. Cameron settled on top of Paul, his hands slipping down over his dress shirt.

Paul's hands slid upward. He tugged at the hem of his T-shirt. They broke their kiss long enough for him to toss it off. Paul's dress shirt came next then his khaki pants got pulled off. Cameron's PJ pants came off, and the smaller man's hands went to his length, fondling him.

Cameron kissed his lover as his fingers stroked him through his briefs. He could feel his hard length, and he wanted to have a look at his sizable cock. "Can I take these off?" he asked playfully, tugging at the waistband.

Paul nodded and gasped when Cam went for a sensitive part on his neck, licking and sucking. "God, yes."

The material fell away, and he worked his way down Paul's

body. He had the typical swimmer's build, lean and muscled. Cam loved it—although they were close to the same height, he outweighed Paul by a good fifty pounds.

His chin bumped against Paul's uncut cock, and then the hard member bounced against his lips. He inhaled the deep musky scent, nuzzling before taking him into his mouth. The older man tasted just how he thought he would—a hint of salt, but not overly strong or offensive. He tasted like heaven. Cameron worked on deep-throating him.

His lover's fingers brushed through his hair, holding on as he worked him over with his mouth. "I need you," he growled. "I need to fuck you."

Cameron pulled off and jerked away like he had been scalded. "I don't. I haven't...."

Paul's thick cock jutted out and stood against his stomach. He inched closer to him, and reaching out, he pulled Cameron close to him, kissing him. "It's okay, I won't hurt you."

He stiffened. "I don't bottom." He might enjoy fucking men, but he wasn't gay—so he wasn't a bottom.

His lover pulled him close, kissing him again. "I need to claim you as mine," he said, between kisses. "Dreamworld, remember?"

His breath came in short bursts. Dreamworld—no rules, no consequences. He knew he would give in to Paul. Something about him had him enraptured.

The smaller man pushed him onto the bed and covered his body with his own. Their hard cocks pressed against each other. Working his way down, he stopped when his lips were level with Cameron's thick member. Paul used his mouth like something out of a porno. He moved again, licking and teasing his heavy sack. Paul pushed his legs apart, his tongue seeking even lower.

Cameron let out a hearty groan as his lover's tongue connected with the sensitive flesh. He growled low and long, bucking his hips. No one had ever rimmed him before. He'd rimmed plenty of guys, but he never let anyone reciprocate, always figuring it was the first step to them fucking him. He shivered with anticipation.

A slick finger slipped inside of him with ease. Paul sucked on his cock, rolling the foreskin around with his mouth. A second finger joined the first, brushing against his sweet spot. He cried out, kicking his legs out, forcing his cock deeper down Paul's throat.

He kept teasing him with his fingers, working him over. It wasn't until Cameron growled and begged Paul to fuck him that he stopped. He gave one last lick to the thick purple head of Cameron's cock before sliding along the length of his body. Their mouths met in a hot kiss, their tongues battling for dominance as he widened his knees and his lover settled between them.

Paul pressed into him, but Cameron stopped him. "Condom? Lube?"

"Dreamworld, remember? No condoms needed." Paul brushed his fingers through his hair.

"What about lube?"

He laughed, low and sexy. "We don't need that either. Our minds are basically having sex with each other, Cam. Since we're not physically touching, we don't need anything to make the movement easier. So relax, I'm not going to hurt you."

Paul pushed into him with not even a hint of resistance. Cameron sighed as his older lover fully sheathed inside of him.

"You feel amazing," he admitted. It felt so good to have Paul connect with him. Even the slightest movement meant his lover's hard cock brushed against his prostate.

He moved slowly and gently, but they built up to a quick and frantic rhythm. Cameron clung to Paul, holding them together.

"I'm not sure if I can hold on." He moaned as Paul increased his pace. "I'm going to come."

The other man buried his face in Cameron's neck. "That's it," he whispered. "Come for me. I need to feel you." Paul bit hard on a spot at the base of his neck, sucking hard.

He squeezed a hand between them and managed to add in a few extra tugs of his cock, which helped to send him tumbling over the edge. He clung to his lover, calling his name.

Paul growled, his lover screaming into him as his thrust

became erratic, and he collapsed onto him, gasping.

They collapsed together in a sticky heap, not wanting to move, not wanting to break the spell. His heart raced through everything, his body and mind complete.

Paul pulled out and moved to one side, his head resting on Cameron's chest. "That was amazing, even for dream sex."

Cameron ran his fingers through his lover's long, sweaty, boyish blond hair. He inhaled, relishing in the musky scent of another male.

"It was very good."

Paul stared at Cameron, his thick-lashed green eyes blinking. "You need to get some sleep."

He yawned in response. "I'm not tired."

"Not now, but you can't stay awake in the Dreamworld forever. If you do, you'll be exhausted in the morning." Paul moved higher and kissed Cameron one last time. "Sleep. I'll see you tomorrow night," he promised. He rolled to one side, giving him some room.

Cameron rolled over, draping his arm over his new partner's waist, pulling him closer.

"Night," he whispered in Paul's ear.

Chapter Nine

Cameron awoke much the same as he had the morning before, half-hard and with stickiness in his PJ pants, telling him he had had another wet dream—sort of. At least he remembered it this time. He stretched in bed, finding it empty with Jaden nowhere to be seen. He could hear the water running in the sink in the bathroom, and he assumed she would be in there. He blocked her. She didn't need to hear his thoughts.

He rolled the night over in his mind. The realization he'd had sex with his partner, even in the Dreamworld, and was made to forget did not sit well with him. Jaden had always been off limits to him, but he wanted her more than anything, and he knew she wanted him, at least in Dreamworld. The shower turned on as he moved out of bed. The idea of her wet and naked in the shower made his morning-semi grow significantly. He wanted her.

Strolling into bathroom as she hadn't bothered to lock the door; he saw her through the frosted glass door, turned away from him, not paying attention to the world outside her shower.

Cam stripped off his T-shirt and PJ pants, tossing them into the corner of the bathroom. He waited. She still hadn't noticed him. He pulled open the shower door and stepped into the steam. Jaden turned, jumped away from him, and let out a high-pitch shriek.

She landed a fist into his chest. He brought down his block enough so he could hear her.

"*What the fuck do you think you're doing?*" she screamed at him. "*You terrified me!*"

Cameron pulled her into his arms, her skin slick and wet beneath his fingers. "I'm claiming what's mine."

He growled low and bent his head enough to capture her mouth. She resisted him at first, pushing her hands against him. He grasped both of her wrists with one hand, holding her, while he kissed her.

She whimpered, giving in to his insistent lips. His partner opened to him, his body covered hers, crushing her into the cool shower tile. His erection pressed against her hip, and he ran his hands over her body, pinching her nipples as she hissed with pleasure. One hand slid lower, seeking her wet heat.

Jaden jolted as her found her round hard nub and groaned at his gentle circling touch.

"I know about the Dreamworld."

She froze and pushed him away. He let her go.

"*How the hell do you know about the Dreamworld?*"

He could feel her panic, near terror, at his words. "*Paul told me last night.*"

He reached out for her, the spray from the shower bouncing off his chest, wanting to comfort her.

"*He had no right to tell you anything.*" She moved toward the shower door. If she bolted, he might lose her. He placed himself between her and the door.

"*Darling, I had every right to know. You can't make amazing, sweet love to me and make me forget it.*"

"*The real world and the Dreamworld are two different things.*" Jaden's hair lay plastered to her head, tendrils of water running down her face.

"*Tell me you don't want me.*"

"*I don't want you,*" she replied too quickly.

He took a step forward, one arm stretched out, blocking her escape. "*Liar.*"

Bending his head again, he captured her lips. She kissed him right away, soft sounds escaping from her mouth.

He reached around her, gripping her beautiful behind and lifting her until she wrapped her legs around his waist. Cameron held her hard against the shower wall, the spray beating down his back.

"Tell me you don't want me." He buried his face in her neck.

"*I don't want you, Cameron.*" Her mental voice dropped a few decibels, somehow sounding huskier. "*I need you.*"

"Christ.... Do you know how much I want you, Jay?"

She laughed. "*I do have an idea.*"

He pulled her down, intending to take her right there, but she stopped him.

"*We need to be safe.*"

"*Please tell me you have something*" He set her onto the floor, struggling to regain some form of control. He wanted her— no, he *needed* her. *Right now.*

Jaden shook her head, water flinging off her hair. "*I've never needed anything before.*" Her skin flushed all the way down between her breasts.

"*Darling, are you telling me you've never done this before?*"

He ached at the thought. After her antics in Dreamworld, it never occurred to him she might be a virgin in the waking world.

"*Not while awake.*"

Groaning, he reached around her to turn the shower off. "You're killing me, Jaden."

After shoving the shower door open, he stepped out, leaving her trembling against the tile. He grabbed a towel, running it over his hair before wrapping it around his waist, hiding his obvious attraction to her. Then he gathered two towels more and pulled Jaden from the shower. He draped one around her and dried her hair with the other.

She scrunched his nose at him. "*I'm capable of drying myself off.*"

"*I know.*" He planted a kiss on her scrunched nose.

He pulled the towel from her hair then scooped her into his

arms. She shrieked and flung her arms around his neck. He carried her into the bedroom and dropped her gently.

"*Cameron.*" She laughed as she bounced on the bed.

"*Stay here, I'll be right back.*" He kissed her one more time before he went to dig through his go-bag. In the bottom, he found the emergency condom and a lube sampler he had thrown in the bag ages ago. Not expired—*thank God.*

Rejoining his partner in the bed, he removed the remaining towel from her then kissed her as he moved down her body. His mouth captured one of her nipples, his fingers playing with the other one. She gasped and arched against him.

He traced over her stomach with his fingertips then went lower toward her sex She jumped as he touched her there, his fingers just ghosting over her clitoris.

"*Touch me, Cam, please.*"

He rubbed his thumb over her, enjoying her responsive sounds. He smiled, moving lower. Kissing his way down, he headed for the ultimate prize. Cameron blew on her softly, making her whimper, before he tasted her, his tongue making broad strokes around the hard nub.

Jaden opened herself more to him, widening her legs. She tasted warm and sweet, and she cried out as he eased a finger inside of her.

He kissed her inner thigh. "Shhh," he soothed.

He hooked his digit upward, searching for her sweet spot. When he found it, she made a high-pitched noise in the back of her throat, not a mental noise, but one she made without thinking. He loved it.

He slid a second finger in, she felt so tight. He licked and sucked on her hard clit.

"*Please, Cam, I need you.*" She tugged on his damp hair.

He smiled at her, moving his tongue over her one last time. "*Are you sure, Jaden?*"

"*I've never been surer about anything.*" Her fingers wound their way in his hair. "*I need you, Cameron.*"

He slipped his fingers away from her and reached for the

condom and lube sampler. He ripped the top of both items off with his teeth, and added some lube, before rolling the condom on, adding the rest over the latex sheath.

Cam covered Jaden's body with his, staring into her dark-green eyes.

"Talk to me." He brushed the flyaway hair out of her face. "You're in control. If you want me to stop, just say so."

She nodded. He ached to be inside of her, to just throw her down and take her until she moaned his name. He wouldn't, though. He'd take his sweet time with her. She deserved the best for her first waking experience.

Jaden guided his member into her. She whimpered as he slid into her.

"All right?" He stopped just inside her, letting her get used to his size.

"*You're huge.*"

"Sorry."

"*That wasn't a complaint.*" She stroked his face.

He leaned down and kissed her as he slid the rest of the way into her. She gasped and arched against him, her breath coming in short bursts.

He waited for her. Staying still except for the pulsing of his cock, he didn't dare move. When she flexed her hips, squirming beneath him, all but begging him to move, he did—slowly at first.

"You feel amazing, Jay."

She moaned and nodded, her body moving with his. He could already feel his climax building.

"*Please, Cam, more.*"

He increased the power in his thrusts, holding back, not wanting to hurt her, and not wanting to come just yet. She demanded more, though—with her body and her mind, her fingers raking down his spine, forcing him to lose control. She pushed him over the edge, and he screamed her name as he came. She followed suit right behind him.

Cameron collapsed his full weight onto her, his breath coming in short pants, unable to move. Jaden pushed on him.

"Can't breathe."

He slipped out of her and rolled to one side, pulling her on top of him.

"Sorry, darling." He kissed her sweaty hair. *"I forget how tiny you are."*

She clicked her teeth at being called tiny but didn't say anything. Instead, her fingers traced over his chest and neck, the focus on one spot at the base.

"Did I bite you?" She traced a spot. *"You have a bite mark on your neck."*

Shit. Paul. *"Uh, maybe."*

Jaden jerked away like she had been slapped. *"What about Paul?"* She scrambled backward, wrapping a sheet around her chest.

Fuck. He had lost his block somewhere in the middle of sex. *"Babe."*

"Did you sleep with Paul?" Her mental voice trembled. *"In Dreamworld?"*

"I did, but it was only after he told me about you, about us. About the mate thing," Cameron said.

"What mate thing?" Her eyes narrowed.

Shit, Shit, Shit, she didn't know.

"I don't know what? *Cameron. Stop lying to me."*

He wrapped the comforter around his waist. "I don't.... I can't explain it." He struggled to explain the information he had just received, and in Dreamworld at that. *"I'm sorry, Jaden. You'll have to ask Paul."*

She huffed at him and got off of the bed, storming into the living room, the sheet trailing behind her. He considered following her, but stopped himself. Instead, he went to the bathroom, getting rid of the used condom. He felt a little sick when he saw the streaks of blood on the outside. *Dammit.* He had hurt her, and, instead of cuddling her and making her feel special after her first time, they had gotten into a fight about him dream-banging her protector. Fuck it all to hell.

He washed and pulled on a clean pair of PJ pants before

joining her in the living room. She sat on the couch with the sheet still wrapped around her. Her laptop sat open in front of her, but her eyes were closed as though she wanted to reach someone outside her usual range.

The coffee maker had brewed automatically this morning, and he got himself a cup, waiting for her to talk to whomever she was trying to reach. He sat at the high counter, sipping on his too-warm coffee, when her eyes snapped open and she started typing away on the laptop.

"It's almost one in the morning here, Jay," an accented voice said from the computer. "This had better be good."

"*Of course it is.*"

Her fingers clicked furiously on keys. She glared at Cameron, and he joined her on the couch. Her screen blinked the icon for her video-chat program for a few moments then Paul appeared on the screen. He looked almost like he had in Dreamworld—except his mussed hair as if he had been asleep, and there were a few more laugh lines around his eyes.

Paul's gaze flicked to the side of the screen where he sat.

"Oh." He blushed. "Hi, Cameron."

"*What did you tell him last night?*" Cameron could hear her thoughts as she typed. "*What did you tell him about mates?*"

Paul pressed his lips together. "Nothing."

"*You might be halfway across the world, Paul, but I know when you're lying. Tell me now.*" Jaden pulled the sheet a little tighter around herself. Whatever this meant to her, it bothered her, in more ways than one.

"Jaden, it's not fair to you if I tell you." He ran his fingers though his thick blond hair.

"*It was fair to tell Cameron, but it's not fair to tell me?*"

"I'm sorry, luv. I am really. You need to figure this out on your own, but Cameron needed to know."

"*I need to know, Paul.*"

The tired sounding, heavily accented voice replied, "No, you don't."

Jaden turned to glared at him and then turned back to the

man on the screen. "*Why did you sleep with him?*"

Paul opened his mouth, gasped, and started to deny it, but a scowl from Jaden silenced him. "It just happened, Jay."

"*I'm not an idiot.*"

He didn't say anything.

"*Is Cameron my mate?*"

"I don't know."

"*Is he your mate?*"

Paul glanced over at him, pure longing on his face. "He might be."

"*Was he Adeline's mate?*"

Paul chewed his lower lip. "Yes."

Jaden pounded her fist on the coffee table.

"*Dammit, Paul, how many times do I have to tell you I'm not Adeline?*" She stabbed at the keys.

"I know you're not."

"*Stop meddling in my life, Paul.*"

"I'm just trying to help."

"*You're not helping. I'm not fifteen anymore. I need a chance to run my own life. You need to butt out. Stay away from me and stay away from Cameron. I can't do this anymore.*" Jaden snapped the laptop closed. She turned and glowered at him. "*Paul forgets I'm not his dead sister and I'm not a kid anymore. Don't let his misunderstandings guide you. I hope you'll understand if I want to pretend this morning never happened.*"

"Jay—"

"*I need to shower. We're going to be late. Call Ruth and make up some excuse.*" She stood and hurried into the bathroom, the sheet trailing behind her.

Cameron's shoulders slumped, his heart totally broken. For the first time, he had answers to why he always found himself unhappy in relationships. He had believed Paul about him and Jaden being mates—how telepaths had one true mate, and how he would be lucky enough to have two mates. Parts of his life were at last making sense and they had been snatched away.

He took a few deep breaths. They were both going to be late

for work. He composed himself enough to call Ruth and get her to cover for them. After Jaden emerged from the bathroom, wrapped in a towel, he took his turn in the shower—alone. He couldn't help but think this was the last time he would ever be this close to Jaden. He could already sense her mental barriers, long broken down between them, rebuilding and keeping him out for what he feared would be an eternity.

Chapter Ten

By the time they walked into the Special Crimes Unit, Jaden appeared to be her normal, attitude-filled self. Cameron still felt a little lost in regard to what happened that morning, but he had to be professional enough to push it aside and focus on the case at hand—at least for the moment.

They had a few hours remaining to build their case against Meincke before their appointment with Internal Affairs at one o'clock—then they would have to turn everything they had against Meincke over to them. Ruth had done some digging. Meincke's apartment on the west side didn't offer him enough privacy or space to be able to keep the girls. Also, the image Emily had sent Jaden placed her in a basement of some sort. If he was the perp, as Cameron feared, then he had to have another property somewhere to keep the girls.

The admin assistant at the front showed them into a room where Meincke and Leann had already spread out everything CSU had collected so far and processed from the Jenkins' home.

"About time you joined us." Meincke glanced over from a computer. A video of a girl being abused by Jenkins played on the screen. Cam turned away, and Meincke stopped the video. "Sorry," he apologized, "I forget how hard the images are to look at when you're not used to seeing them."

"It's okay. What do we have?" He took a chair next to Leann as she organized loose photos into sets.

Jaden sat across from them, separating herself from the other three. She pulled out her laptop and turned it on—her way of appearing busy when she wanted to work on reading their minds.

"CSU is still processing." Leann met Cameron's gaze. "So far, they've found trace semen samples on several photographs. They'll run the DNA to see if it matches Jenkins. Also, his fingerprints are all over most of the photos along with one or two unknowns. They're running them through AFIS now to see if they can come up with anything." She handed him a sheet of paper outlining what she had just said. "Tech is still working on the computer. Appears there are a number of partitions with a 512 bit encryption code."

"Is that a lot?" Cameron admittedly wasn't as computer savvy as some of the other officers on the force.

Leann shrugged, but Jaden replied. "*It is when you consider the government only uses 128 bit encryption code.*"

He nodded to tell her he got her message but didn't offer a response. "What kind of charges are we looking at?"

"Well, every image is a separate charge. We have over a hundred here, and CSU probably has, including the albums, another two hundred and fifty or more." Leann had a running tally on the papers in front of her.

"Plus, each of the videos he made is one count production of child pornography," Meincke added. "The techs digitized the videos so we can go through them easier, and it preserves the images as well. Not to mention anything else we find on the laptop."

"I called in Internet Sex Crimes as well. They might have seen some of these images or videos before if they've made it to the web. Can help us trace who he's been sharing images with," Leann said. "They also keep a record of all images we collect in case they come across them during a later investigation. The database means they won't be chasing down images to find the producer as we've already shut him down."

"They can't go after him again?" he replied.

"No, we can only nail him once for production and distribution. It's a tragedy these guys make this stuff and upload it to the Internet. Every time the images of these children are downloaded and viewed they're victimized again. We can nail them for possession, but the sentences are far too light."

"They're too light for all sex crimes against children. Raping your daughter for ten years? Gets you six months' probation and a hundred and fifty hours doing community service—get this— with kids." Meincke shook his head.

"I can't tell if he's happy about the sentences or genuinely upset. He's a bitch to try and get a read on, Cam." Jaden's fingers clicked away on her laptop as she took notes on whatever was going on in their minds, his included.

"Sounds like bull," he agreed. "We arrested him for the assault on one victim. When can we bring these additional charges?"

"I've already done the paperwork for the first hundred and twenty or so charges. He's arraigned at two today. I think the prosecutor is going to ask for remand until we know the full extent of the charges."

They worked for another ten minutes. *"I think Meincke has a second property."*

Cameron grabbed the edge of the table so he didn't startle, he shot her a sideways glance. *"Huh?"*

"He has a house, outside of the city. I'll e-mail Ruth. It's important."

"You think?"

"If he's the perp, and God I fucking hope he's not, that's where the girls are."

"Get Ruth on it." He returned to cataloging at photos with the other detective.

Another thirty minutes passed before Leann's phone rang. "Detective Steele, Special Crimes Unit."

"Black tea," Jaden said.

"It's Detective Muller from Internet Crimes. He's on his way over but stopping for coffee. Would you like anything?" she asked.

"My usual," Meincke replied.

"I'll have a black coffee, large. Jaden, you want a large black tea right?" Cameron asked, and she nodded, pretending to be absorbed in her computer.

Leann passed on the orders to Detective Muller. "Excellent. We need a few more eyes on this case. I can't believe how long this has been going on. We pulled the files from our complaints alone. They've had foster kids for twelve years. In that time, eighteen complaints, all said to be unfounded by CPS."

"*Fuck me in the ass,*" Jaden shot over to him.

Cameron had to stop himself from snickering as she used Ruth's favorite swear phrase.

"I think we need to re-open all of the investigations," he replied.

"Agreed. We might have to get some CPS investigators involved as well." She added a note to the things she had written on the pad in front of her.

She showed Cameron how they were cataloguing the photos, and he went to work. Fifteen minutes later, two men walked in the room, both carrying a tray laden with coffees and a box of donuts.

"Hi, Chris. Thanks, you didn't have to get donuts." Leann took the box from one of the detectives and placed it on an empty side table, away from any evidence.

"No problem, Lee." He set the coffees on the table and stuck out his hand. "Chris Muller and my partner, Logan Weber," Muller said. Cam gave them a quick once over. They were both blond, blue eyes, tall, and well built. Interesting.

"*Oh, come on. They're so sleeping with each other. I could tell that without reading their minds.*"

Cameron shook his head at her. "Nice to meet you." He offered his hand to Chris. "Cameron Olsen, this is my partner, Jaden Black." He gestured toward her.

Muller shook it, and Weber set down the coffees he carried

and shook his hand as well. Logan passed take-out cups to Leann and Meincke. "Black tea?" he asked, holding a large cup.

"It's Jaden's," Cameron replied.

"Oh, here." He brought it to her, setting it next to her computer. "There's milk and sugar in the bag if you're interested."

She nodded, pretending to ignore him rather than lip-sync and risk giving away her secret. Cameron took his coffee from Muller and thanked him. Leann caught the pair up on everything they had found. Chris went to viewing the videos with Meincke while Logan worked on the other side of the table next to Jaden.

Webber picked out several photos he'd seen before he pulled out his laptop and opened their database for references to see if they had an identified manufacturer or not. They started to review each of the flagged photographs. Many were of unknown origin, and it appeared they had been produced by Jenkins. After about an hour and a half of staring at the images, Cameron excused himself. He used the bathroom and meant to step out of the building, not only to clear his head, but to also call Ruth in private. Except when he exited the washroom, Chris stood there, waiting, and grabbed him by the elbow.

"Walk with me." The younger detective steered him toward the elevators.

His odd behavior intrigued Cameron enough that he nodded and followed him without protest. They passed through the cubical farm in silence and stepped onto a full elevator.

"*Jay.*" Cameron waited as the elevator descended, but he didn't get an answer. "*Jaden,*" he mentally screamed at her.

"*What?*"

"*Listen in on this for me.*"

"*Sure.*"

He stepped off the elevator on the ground floor and followed the other detective out into the late summer sunshine. He fell into step next to him. Muller didn't speak until they were a good block away from the building. "I need you to tell me something, and I need you to be honest."

"Alright."

"Are you investigating Meincke?" he asked.

Cameron replied with care. "What makes you think that?"

"Are you or aren't you?" Muller snapped.

He shook his head. "I can't confirm or deny that statement."

"That's a very nice way of saying yes," the younger man replied. "Have you brought this to Internal Affairs yet?"

"I can't say anything, sorry."

"You haven't, but you're going to. Later today most likely." Chris walked away from the building. Fuck, he sounded like a mind reader. "I'm not a mind reader, don't worry," he added. "Jaden is the only one of those on the force, at least that IA knows about."

"Do you like answering your own questions?" Cameron asked sarcastically.

"I'll be honest with you if you're honest with me—and trust me when I say this—you want me on your team." He led them into a small green space.

"*Tell him,*" Jaden interjected.

Chris chose a bench, and Cameron sat next to him. He blew out a breath. He wasn't sure what the other detective's angle was, but he trusted Jaden, and if she wanted him to know, then so be it.

"We started this investigation with the disappearance of Marissa Preston." He watched as some kids ran around the play area on the other side of the park. "We managed to connect Marissa's disappearance with another little girl from about six months ago. They could be sisters they were that identical, so we decided to see if there were any more girls matching their description."

"How many?" Chris asked.

"Six, over the last three and a half years, including Marissa we think. We searched for common factors. Three of the girls were in the same foster home and reported abuse at the Jenkins's house. The older sister of one of the girls was abused there as well. She gave us enough for the search warrant. We found the kiddie porn, called in Special Crimes. They called you in."

Muller stared at the playground, he took a deep breath. "How did you end up investigating Meincke?"

"Connections. The only link between all of the missing girls was they all made reports about abuse to the Special Crimes Unit, and Meincke and Steele were assigned to their cases. Heck, we weren't even sure until Jaden caught him snapping photos of some of Jenkin's images and even then...." He shrugged.

"Fuck." He shook his head. "You don't think...?" He narrowed his eyes. "Of course you do. Why else would you be here? Dammit." He kicked the dirt in front of the bench. Standing, he paced in front of him. "This is so much worse than they thought. So much worse. Three and a half years. Fuck."

"I spilled my guts. It's your turn."

The younger man blew out a deep breath. "We've been investigating him for keeping unauthorized images, and Steele reported it. She's not as clueless as she appears. Took us over a year to get integrated with them." He shook his head. "I need to make some phone calls."

"You're Internal Affairs?"

Chris nodded while dialing his phone.

"We're an undercover unit, working for Internet Crimes and Internal Affairs at the same time. Yeah, it's Muller. We got a huge problem."

"*Did you get that?*" he asked Jaden.

"*Loud and clear. There's more he's not telling you. I'm sure of it. Something about Logan.*"

"*I'll work on it.*"

"Yeah, thanks. Bye." Chris jabbed at his phone. "Your afternoon appointment with IA has been cancelled. We're working together on this from now on."

"Fine, but I want to be filled in the rest of the way."

Muller nodded for him to follow, and they re-traced their steps toward the building.

"We don't have much. We've planted viruses on his computer. He's smart. Anything he has isn't hooked into the

Internet," Chris replied. "We know he's borrowed and returned over a thousand images and videos. We think he's got a separate machine just for that. There are never any fingerprints or DNA on the images he takes. His apartment is clean, so we think he's got another location."

"We've come to the same conclusion. If he's taking these girls, then he needs a private space for them," Cameron said. "Have you had any luck finding anything?"

Chris shook his head. "Nothing in his name anyway."

"Ruth was doing some digging. I think Jaden sent her some info she got off Meincke. Let me call her. She might have something."

"Go ahead." They stopped a block or so away from the office, and he dialed Ruth's main line.

"Hello, my lovely, you must be the mind reader in the bunch! I was just about to call you." Ruth's voice bounced over phone line.

"Please, tell me you have something."

"I have a lot of something. Let's begin with Internal Affairs is already investigating Meincke."

"I know. Fast forward. Properties? Other locals? Give me something I can use," Cameron barked.

"Fine, but you'll miss my genius. Anyway, Jaden was right. He owns a farmhouse about an hour away from his apartment. Looks like it used to belong to a grandparent. The utilities are listed in the names of his kids," she replied.

"Hang on." He relayed the information to Muller, who then got on his phone.

"We're going to see if we have enough for the local PD to execute a search warrant for us," Chris told him.

Cameron repeated the information to Ruth. "Okay, sounds good. I e-mailed all the details to you and Jaden, so she would be updated as well. Give me a shout if you need me."

"Thanks, Ruth." He hung up, but the younger detective still spoke in rapid fire, terse sentences on the phone. Cameron waited until he disconnected as well. "Plan?"

"I think we've got enough for a search warrant. One of the other IA teams is writing it up and will coordinate with Ruth. We're to go back and act as normal as possible." He glanced at his watch. "I'm going to suggest we go out for lunch. If it all goes well when we return to the office, IA will arrest him before he gets into the building," Chris said, strategizing. "It's better than trying to do it in the building with a hundred other cops around, trust me."

"Sounds good."

They made their way into the building, Cameron entering first.

"About time you got back." Leann glanced up from the photographs when he re-entered the room. "CSU just dropped off another box of photos."

"Sorry, I had to take a phone call from a witness from another case. You know how that can be."

Leann nodded. "Yeah, I've been there."

Muller returned about five minutes after Cameron. "Sorry," he apologized. "It was the doctor about Noel."

"How's he doing?" Logan asked.

Chris frowned.

Leann leaned over to him. "Chris' son has leukemia," she said in a hushed tone. "We all give him a break when it comes to things, you know?"

"Of course."

He glanced at the young detective. *One hell of a cover for him to come up with.* It left him wondering if there really was a kid, or if he just used it as an excuse.

"*If that's not a load of bull. Kid has been fine for months.*"

Cameron glared at his partner. They kept working with their heads down for the rest of the morning.

Chris stood and stretched his arms wide at twelve-thirty, giving an exaggerated yawn. "What do you say we go grab some lunch? I'm starving."

"I think that's a great idea," Cameron agreed. "Jaden?"

She nodded.

"I don't know. We have an awful lot of work." Leann glanced

at the table of half-catalogued pictures.

"Come on, Lee. We've been at this since eight. I think we need a break." Meincke stretched his legs.

"Agreed," Logan added. "It will still be here when you get back, Lee."

She hesitated, unsure, but three men giving her puppy-dog eyes made her cave. "Fine, but make sure one of the CSU techs comes here to watch the evidence while we're gone."

One of the techs, who'd already had lunch, volunteered, and Cam followed the group out of the building and down the street to a popular steak place.

They got seated quickly, and the waitress came to take drink orders.

"*Coke*," Jaden told Cam.

The others ordered. "Two cokes," he said, indicating himself and his partner.

The girl left to get their drinks.

"Do you ever say anything?" Leann asked Jaden. "I don't think I've heard you say a word since I've met you."

Jaden shrugged and gave him a quick but meaningful glance.

"She doesn't like to talk around new people." He brushed off the question.

Leann raised an eyebrow. "No offense, but you're one of youngest cops and the youngest detective I've ever met. How the heck did you make detective if you don't talk around new people?"

Jaden pressed her lips together in a tight line "*Help.*"

"Look, Leann, we've got a ninety-eight percent solve rate on our cases," Cameron pointed out. "Jaden is a great investigator. She went into the academy right out of school and made her bones early on the serial rape case over in the brewery district. Jaden pretty much single-handedly took down the suspect by working her ass off. She doesn't talk because...." He pretended to hesitate. Everything he'd said had been the truth so far. Time to add in a tiny lie, so the whole truth didn't get out. "She stutters around new people. It took her three months before she would talk to me instead of through Ruth."

"Oh I...." Leann blanched. "I'm sorry. I didn't mean to pry."

Jaden replied with a shrug as if to say it was okay.

Logan asked Chris about Noel, and the conversation switched that way, avoiding the awkward silence. The rest of lunch flew by, and, less than an hour later, they found themselves walking toward the office.

They were almost to the main doors when two men in matching dark-blue suits approached the group.

"Matthew Meincke?" one said, staring hard at the four men in the group.

"Yes?" He stepped forward.

They both flashed their badges at him. "Keep your hands where we can see them," the taller one instructed. One approached him, and removed Meincke's side arm, handing it to the other, who secured it. "Put your hands behind your back."

He did.

"What am I being arrested for?" Meincke asked. He glanced around wildly for an escape route.

"I am arresting you for the kidnapping and confinement of Marissa Preston. It is my duty to inform you that you have the right to retain and instruct counsel without delay. You may call any lawyer you want. There is a 24-hour telephone service available, which provides a legal aid duty lawyer who can give you legal advice in private. This advice is given without charge, and the lawyer can explain the legal aid plan to you. If you wish to contact a legal aid duty lawyer, I can provide you with a telephone number. Do you understand?"

Meincke nodded, his jaw set, eye twitching.

"Do you want to call a lawyer?"

Meincke nodded again.

"You are not obliged to say anything, but anything you do say may be given in evidence." He led Meincke toward the cruiser.

Leann blinked, slack jawed as they led him away. She turned toward the others. "What the hell just happened?"

Chapter Eleven

*A*nother set of IA officers escorted Leann away, explaining as they went.

"They found Marissa?" Cam asked Logan and Muller.

Logan nodded. "About twenty minutes ago. I got the message on my phone while we were at lunch. They're taking her to the children's hospital for evaluation. It looks like he was keeping her in the basement of his grandparent's old house. CSU is just arriving now to comb the property to see what evidence they can turn up."

Relief flood Cameron, a weight he no longer had to carry floated off his shoulders.

"*Has Marissa's mother been told yet?*" Jaden asked.

Cam didn't blink, but the other two men jumped at the realization they could hear Jaden as if she was talking, but her lips didn't move.

"Uh, no. We thought you two would like to do that." Muller exchanged a stare with his partner, and they both glanced at Jaden, slightly shocked. "You've been the primaries, and we thought it would be better for her mom if you brought her the news."

"Thank you." He glanced at his watch, almost one-thirty. "What about all of the evidence we collected from the Jenkins's home?"

"We'll finish what we can and hand it off to another team who will do the rest. The most important thing is you reunite mother and daughter."

"*Agreed,*" Jaden said.

They shook hands and followed the pair inside, heading down to the parking garage. Jaden drove them over to Cindy Preston's apartment.

"*That was rather interesting, don't you think?*" she said, once they were out of the building and into traffic.

"Why?"

"*Zero to sixty in thirty seconds,*" she replied.

"Overwhelming to say the least," he agreed.

Jaden navigated through the early afternoon traffic. He could feel the nervous but excited energy rolling off her as she drove. She went through a red light, failing to activate her lights, almost causing an accident.

"Watch out will you?" he snapped at her, the emotions Jaden projected to him took from his own. His whole mind overwhelmed with happiness and sadness at once, tension between them flaring and then bubbling down in almost an instant.

She took a deep breath and peeked at him over her should as she continued driving. "*How do you want to handle telling Cindy?*"

"Nice subject change. How about, 'Hey Cindy, your daughter is alive.'"

"*Don't be an ass.*" She clicked her teeth at him. "*You know what I meant.*"

"Tell her that her daughter is alive. Then break the news she was sexually assaulted, or at least I'm assuming she was. Then when the dust settles, tell her it was a cop. Good plan?" he quipped.

"Yeah, you're an ass. I'll do it," Jaden replied. She glared at him when they stopped at a red light.

"*What's that supposed to mean?*"

"You know exactly what it means." Jaden threw the SUV around the corner into the complex where Cindy Preston lived. *"Just keep quiet. I'll do the talking."*

"In a manner of speaking."

Jaden shot him the death scowl and clicked her teeth. Fuckin' eh, they never had strain like this between them.

She parked in front of the building and jumped out of the SUV in a flash with Cameron trailing behind her. She waited until he pressed the buzzer.

"Hello?" Cindy answered.

"Cindy, it's Detectives Olsen and Black. Can we come in?"

"Sure, hold on." She buzzed them in. They all but ran up the stairs to her apartment. "What's going on?" she asked when she opened the door to them.

She wore a pair of PJ pants and an oversized sweater, her hair piled on top of her head in a mess, and the trails of makeup left on her face were smeared. She looked like hell.

"Are you off work today?" Jaden murmured as Cindy showed them inside.

"I have the next three days off on the rotation. What's going on?" She glanced warily between the two detectives.

"Come, sit down," she offered.

Cindy shook her head, standing in the middle of the kitchen. "Just tell me."

"We found Marissa."

She collapsed onto the floor. "Oh, God!"

He dropped down and gathered her in his arms. "She's alive, Cindy. Marissa is alive," he told her over and over again until the words seemed to sink in.

"She's alive?"

"Yes," Jaden replied, lip-syncing her words. *"She's on her way to the children's hospital right now to get checked out. Come on, let's go get dressed."*

She helped Cindy off the floor and into the bedroom. He waited until the two women rejoined him in the kitchen. She appeared a bit more put together, but still had the air of a woman desperate to see her child.

"Let us take you. You shouldn't be driving," he told her.

"All right." They got her coat, and she stuffed her feet into a pair of shoes.

Cameron drove them to the hospital, and Jaden sat in the back with her. He couldn't hear her mind spiel, but from Cindy's side of the conversation, he gathered Jaden was filling her in on the sketchy details they had.

By the time they arrived and checked in with the nurses, Cindy looked like a nervous wreck. The orderly showed them to Marissa's room. Cindy rushed in, hugged her daughter tightly, and together they cried.

୬

Every ounce of energy had been drained from his body by the time Jaden dropped him off at his condo. They had brought Cindy to the hospital and stayed for some questions from her before returning to the office. IA had in turn grilled them for a good two hours before they were free to go home, with the promise of turning over everything they had on Meincke and then some to IA by the following afternoon.

He stopped in the mailroom on his way upstairs, finding his box stuffed, mostly with flyers and a few bills. He threw out the former and dropped the latter onto the small table in the entryway when he got inside to be dealt with tomorrow. They had worked six days straight on this case. They were due for two or three days off before they caught something else. Maybe he could head to his cabin again before he had to shut it down for the winter.

He ate a frozen dinner before crashing out. It didn't even occur to him he had fallen asleep on the couch until he heard his phone ringing.

By the time he managed to get to his cell phone, it had already gone to voicemail. Immediately after, his house phone rang. He answered it, rubbing his hands over his face. "Yeah."

"Detective Olsen?" a female voice asked—it sounded like one of their dispatchers.

"Yeah."

"I'm sorry to wake you, but Detective Lang thought you should be called in on this one," the dispatcher explained. "She asked that you call her as soon as possible."

Cameron groaned. Couldn't he catch a break? "Thanks, what's her number?"

The dispatcher gave it to him, and he keyed it into his cell phone. As soon as she hung with him, he dialed Lang.

"Lang," she answered.

"It's Detective Olsen. You wanted a call." He knew he sounded exhausted, but he didn't care.

"Sorry to call so late," she said.

He glanced at the clock—close to four a.m. "Or very early, depending on who you ask. What's important enough that you needed to call me at this time of the night?"

"I think you and Detective Black need to come see this homicide scene," she said. "It's...well, it's interesting, to say the least."

"Spill, Lang, I'm too tired for bull." He got himself off the couch and walked toward the bathroom, knowing he would go in, whether he wanted to or not.

"If I didn't know any better, I would guess this victim was Detective Black. Not only that, there is a veiled threat toward her," Lang replied.

"Define a veiled threat." Damn, just what they needed, back-to-back messed-up cases.

"It says 'Catch me before I catch you, Black'," Lang explained.

"How do you know it was directed toward Jaden specifically?" His heart skipped a beat at the thought. They'd just gone through the wringer with the Meincke case. The last thing they needed was a threat toward Jaden.

"We don't," Lang admitted. "This chick is a dead ringer for her though. I mean a *dead* ringer. It's the fourth body we've gotten with a similar appearance to her in a month, at least according to Bill Wilson. Also, she's the only Black we have, that's a detective anyway."

"All right, I'll be over there to check it out," he said after a few moments of debate. Wilson had mentioned a floater two days ago to him. Even if the guy was an ass, he had a point. If, in fact, this was the fourth body to pop up to look like Jaden, he needed to go. "Give me the address."

He jotted it down on a scrap piece of paper then disconnected, deciding to wait before he got Jaden involved. After a very quick shower, he dressed in a clean suit and went out the door, running the towel through his hair one more time to make sure it had dried before he made it down to his car.

He arrived at the crime scene forty-five minutes after Lang called.

"About time you got here." She threw the cigarette she had been smoking out into the street.

The detective appeared to be in her mid-to late fifties, with a hard face and over-bleached blonde hair, but her kind eyes told him she hadn't been lost to the job—not yet. He vaguely remembered her from his stint in Homicide.

"We're waiting on the coroner to move the body."

"Is there an ETA?"

"Not yet. Where's your partner?" Lang led him inside the house.

"She'll join us later. She's pretty out of it after our last case," he explained, not wanting to get into details about the ongoing investigation into Meincke.

As they opened the door to the home, the thick scent of blood filled his nose. Fresh, based on the smell, and the way it hung in the air meant there was a lot of it. He donned the protective clothing CSU wore and entered the crime scene.

The room was something out of his worst nightmares; he swallowed the bile rising in his throat as he surveyed the scene. The girl lay posed on the bed, blood soaked the sheets and blankets, and, on the wall, the phrase *Catch me before I catch you, Black* had been written in what appeared to be the victim's blood. He regarded the girl. She did resemble Jaden. It also seemed she'd been made to do so after the fact. Bits of hair on the floor told Cameron the perp had cut her hair to match his partner's reverse bob. Blood covered her lower body, but her face remained clean, covered in flawless style almost identical to the heavy eye makeup Jaden favored. The victim wore a pair of pristine underwear with blood smears underneath.

"He posed her," Cameron said to Lang.

"We think so. The underwear was placed on post mortem. Looks like he might have brought it with him."

He examined the matching bra and panties the victim wore, which were nice. They even seemed a tiny bit familiar, maybe an ex-girlfriend had something similar, but not anything special. "How can you tell?"

"The victim preferred off-shelf budget. Trust me, you can't get that at Wal-Mart," the female CSU tech replied.

"They're designer—definitely—cost at least five, six hundred for the set," Lang agreed.

Cameron regarded them. "If they cost that much, there can only be a few shops in town specializing in them. It should be worth running down."

"If we can get a designer and a model, that will narrow it to maybe a handful. Most high-end lingerie stores keep records of what their customers buy and like so, when more comes in stock, they can notify customers right away."

"I'm not going to ask how you know that."

Lang blushed. "I want to find out if there are any more similarities to Detective Black—besides the obvious."

"Who found her?" he asked.

Lang shook her head. "Anonymous call from a pay phone at a gas station across town. They didn't have any surveillance, but I asked patrol to canvas the area to see if they can get any security footage. It doesn't look hopeful."

"You think the perp called it in?"

"Yeah, he wanted us to find her in perfect condition." She scowled in disgust.

They spent the next hour going over the scene while CSU personnel buzzed around them. The coroner arrived at five to six. She went over the body, bagging the victim's hands for trace evidence, and promised to be careful processing the underwear, in case they got lucky and the perp left some of his DNA behind.

Once she had collected the body, Cameron headed home, telling Lang he would be in touch with Jaden once he caught a few more hours of sleep. Scratch that—he needed a proper week off and a lot more sleep. On the way to his condo, he called Ruth's office line and got her voicemail. He left a message detailing what had been happening and asking her to fill Jaden in, along with sending a pick up for him around ten.

He let himself into his condo, his reserves running on empty. On the way to the bedroom, he stripped out of his clothes then collapsed into bed face first, falling into a deep sleep.

Chapter Twelve

Ringing cell phones had become the bane of his existence. He reached over, feeling around on the table, but couldn't located the offending device. His phone stopped ringing, only to start again. *Dammit.* He found it on the floor, next to his nightstand. "Olsen."

"Sorry to wake you, sweetie," Ruth said. "Lang wants you. She's got some interesting developments on the case."

"Oh?" He rolled over, trying to find the energy to get moving.

"Looks like the underwear the victim was wearing has two DNA samples in it, male and female."

"Right, perp and victim." He slid out from under the covers.

"Nope, unknown female, and a possible plant on the unknown male. It's running through the DNA database now."

"Uh-huh." His brain slowly processed the information. "Wait, it takes at least twenty-four hours to get DNA. How did she get a profile so fast?"

"They're trial testing this new rapid DNA test. We still have to back it up with the traditional methods, but you get results in two to four hours. Anyway, Lang wants you in the office ASAP. I just got an e-mail from Jaden saying she'll be there in forty-five minutes. Is that enough time?"

He had to stop himself from sighing. "Yeah, thanks, Ruth."

After he finished the call, he pulled himself out of bed. His feet hit the floor, and he made his way into the bathroom. He skipped the shower and got dressed, pulling out the last clean suit in the closet. At least his bi-weekly maid and laundry service would be in today, he needed clean suits and underwear.

He got himself together in a decent amount of time and sat at the kitchen counter, eating peanut butter toast with jam when he heard, *"I'm here."*

"Sorry, coming."

He stuffed the last of the toast in his mouth and gulped down the glass of milk he had poured.

"Take your time." Jaden lacked her usual quick-witted attitude.

He grabbed his coat and jogged out to her SUV.

She clicked her teeth at him when he opened the door. *"I told you to take your time."*

He pulled on his seatbelt as she zipped into mid-morning traffic.

"I was ready." A large coffee sat in the holder next to his seat. *"Mine?"*

"Yeah, Lang wants us there an hour ago. It sounds like she got a hit on the DNA."

"That was fast."

"Yeah. It's pretty fucked up, right? Some chick that looks like me. Could be the fourth one. Why wasn't I told?"

"If it is a threat against you, Jay, they're not going to let you investigate. We'll just have to sit on the sidelines." He closed his eyes as Jaden cut off a tractor-trailer, and the driver blew his horn at them. It was just better to not pay attention to all of the near-death moments they had when she drove.

"I know. It just sucks to think someone is dead because of me."

"This isn't about you. Jesus if I thought it was, I would have been at your place last night."

"Why? So you could fuck me again?"

"Dammit, Jay!" Cameron hit the passenger window with his palm. *"It wasn't like that, and you know it."*

Glancing over to him, she flushed, "*I know.*"

She focused on the road, and they were silent for the rest of the drive into the office. They stepped off the elevator on the seventh floor, and the captain of Homicide stood there, his arms crossed.

"Olsen, interview room three." Evan Grigorva scowled at the two of them. "Jaden, interview room five."

Cameron nodded and headed toward the interview rooms, not daring to show a reaction to the captain. Grigorva was not someone to mess with. He examined Jaden's reaction, hoping for a clue as to what had the captain barking at them first thing in the morning.

"*There are security cameras monitoring the doors of your building,*" she said, giving him the only hint as to what was happening.

He entered the room and sat in the chair he usually took during interviews. Grigorva followed him inside and shut the door, taking the spot reserved for suspects. *Interesting.*

"Just to let you know, you're allowed to have a union rep present for this interview." He stared hard at him, his steel-blue eyes unblinking.

"Since I'm not under arrest, and I have nothing to hide, that won't be necessary. Want to tell me what this is about, Captain?" Cameron leaned forward, crossing his arms over his chest. Two could play the intimidation game.

"I need to let you know this interview is being recorded."

Cameron nodded in acknowledgement. *What the hell does he want*?

"Where were you last night between seven p.m. and three a.m.?"

Was he a suspect? Cameron tried to keep a neutral face. "I was in an interview with IA regarding the investigation Detective Black and I closed yesterday. I was there until about eight then she dropped me at home. I got in just before nine. I was home until I received a phone call from Detective Lang at about four a.m. asking me to go out to a homicide scene."

"Did anyone else see you? Did you speak to anyone during that time?" Grigorva questioned.

"The security cameras at my condo building should confirm my timeline. I can call the manager and ask her to send them over."

Thank God for Jaden's reminder about them. He would have forgotten.

"Alright. What about yesterday morning between five a.m. and nine a.m.?"

He shifted uncomfortably. "Detective Black and I were working a case. It was late, so I stayed at her place rather than have her drive me back to mine. She'll tell you the same thing."

"I'm sure she will." He took notes while Cameron waited. He didn't like Grigorva trying to sweat him.

"Look, Captain, I've been very accommodating. I've answered your little questions, but I'm starting to lose my patience. Want to tell me what this is all about?"

They were clearly running something out. Otherwise, he would be in a room with IA rather than the captain in charge of homicide.

Steel-blue eyes regarded him. "Your DNA was recovered at the scene."

"I was at the scene," Cameron point out. "It could have been accidental contamination."

"That's why your DNA was run to begin with, but...." Grigorva leaned in close. "I think Lang would have noticed if you'd 'accidentally' jizzed all over the dead body."

Cameron jerked away as if he had been slapped. "What? You've got to be kidding me." There went his calm demeanor. His heart pounded. *What the hell? How's that possible?*

Grigorva opened the folder and tossed it toward him. He read the report. Semen found at the scene, on the inside of the underwear. Based on the motility of the sperm, they had been deposited approximately twenty-four hours before. There were traces of latex and spermicide in the sample. There was also some of Jaden's DNA mixed in the sample, as well as in the dried vaginal secretions found on the underwear.

"Holy shit." He shook his head.

"I have to ask you this, but did you, uh...ejaculate, between five a.m. and nine a.m. yesterday?" He raised an eyebrow.

"If I did," Cameron said, his voice low and even regaining the cool he had lost, "the exact circumstances are of no relevance to the investigation."

"I have no say in the relationship between you and Detective Black. The only person who does is Chief Novak, and I doubt he will be reading the exact details of any given case."

Cameron wavered. This was not something he wanted revealed to the world—especially since Jaden had decided it was a mistake. But if he didn't admit it, he would look guilty. They already had him dead on the DNA anyway.

"*You can tell him. I already admitted it to Lang. Get this done with,*" Jaden said.

"Detective Black and I had...." He struggled to find the right word. "Relations at her condo yesterday morning."

Grigorva nodded, he had already figured as much.

"Afterward, I threw the condom away in the garbage in her bathroom. Since that's the only, uh...'*deposit*' I've made recently, I suggest you stop this cock-and-bull routine of questioning me and Detective Black and start asking how a perp got into her apartment."

"I agree. I'm sorry to pull you in here on this delicate matter, but we had to cover all of our bases."

Grigorva stood and offered for Cameron to go first through the door. He did, storming out and heading toward the main office area.

He met Jaden in the hall. "*I'm sorry.*"

"Me, too." She nodded toward the unisex bathroom, and Cameron took that as an invite. They stepped in, and she locked the door. "*The underwear on the vic...it was mine. I wore it two days ago.*" Tears sprang in the corner of her eyes. "*The guy who did that, he was in my apartment yesterday.*"

"*I know.*"

Jaden shook, and he reached out and pulled her into his arms.

"It's okay," he whispered into her hair.

"*He could have been there last night, Cameron. I could have been asleep, and he could have been there watching me.*"

A low sob sounded from her chest, and he shushed her, trying to soothe her frazzled nerves.

"*It will be okay, darling. He wasn't there last night. He's not bold enough for that.*"

"*Not yet, but how can I ever go back there now? He was in my house, going through my underwear.*" She shivered.

"*You don't have to. You can stay at my place. It will be okay, Jaden. I promise.*"

"*I wish I could believe you.*"

She clung to him. Cameron did the only thing he could think of. He lowered his head, bending just enough to capture her lips. She didn't resist him, so he kissed her then held her close to his chest for a while. She stood there with her eyes closed, fortifying her world against the onslaught she was about to face.

ೞ

Jaden stood next to him, watching CSU comb through her apartment. Cameron took notes as they tore open the most intimate parts of his partner's life, things even he hadn't seen. Jaden had determined there were two other sets of underwear missing, so two more possible look alike victims. That would bring the total to six dead women. She kept vigil at the breakfast bar as CSU dug through every nook and cranny, searching for some hints as to who had been in her apartment.

Lang came over with a laptop. "The building management just e-mailed the digital security footage. We're hoping someone stands out."

"*Did they figure out how he got in? CSU said the locks didn't appear as though they had been picked.*" Exhausted, she didn't lip sync and just mentally asked.

Lang startled at hearing her mind speak. "Not yet. They have a camera clearly showing your door. Let's see who went in and out of your apartment yesterday." She added with a bit of hesitation, "Uh, how can you...?"

"Jaden's a telepath," Cameron explained. Might as well lay it all out for her. "A very, very powerful one."

"Jesus, I thought the ones on TV were the most powerful ones out there." Lang shook her head. "Can you read my mind?"

Jaden shot him a pained expression. She didn't want to go into full details of her abilities, "Basically, yes she can. You'll get used to it. Can we look at the footage now?"

"Sure. Sorry about that." She set the time for just before they left the condo the previous morning.

"There we go," he said as they emerged from the apartment. Nothing but people walking by then, around eleven, an older Middle-Eastern woman entered Jaden's apartment, carrying bags of what appeared to be groceries.

"That's Ms. Zaher. She's my housekeeper. She comes three times a week. Brings groceries, cooks, does laundry, that kind of stuff. She's like a mom to me."

"How long has she worked for you?" Lang jotted notes.

"For about four years," Jaden admitted. *"Since I moved in here. Paul hired her for me."*

"You moved in here four years ago?" He stared at her, surprised. She would have been about sixteen at the time.

"Yes." She didn't offer any more details. Considering they had been teamed for over two years, he knew very little about his partner.

"Who is Paul?" Lang paused the CCTV footage.

Jaden shot him a meaningful glance. *"He's a friend."*

"How long have you known him?" Lang took more notes.

She thought for a moment. *"Seventeen years or so."*

Lang raised an eyebrow. "How old were you?"

"About three. He's a few years older than me. Childhood friend."

"Does this Paul have a last name? Where does he live?" Lang

scribbled on her pad.

He could feel the panic radiating off Jaden.

"He doesn't have anything to do with this." He tried to get Lang to drop it.

"Cameron, I appreciate you trying to protect your partner, but it's my job to determine that." She turned toward Jaden. "I know it's uncomfortable, being the subject of an investigation, but I need to know this stuff. Something you rule out could be the difference between solving this case and letting a murderer walk."

"Paul Butler. He lives in Sydney, Australia. I had a video chat with him the morning before the murder. Trust me. He was at his flat in Sydney."

Lang nodded and wrote it down. "Thank you."

She turned the video on. They saw a few more people walk past, and about two and a half hours later, Ms. Zaher left. Ten minutes after, a stocky figure appeared on the videotape. He had a hat pulled low over his eyes and avoided the camera. He opened the lock with a key.

Jaden gasped. *"How did he get a key? The only person who has key besides me and Paul is Ms. Zaher."*

"There are several possibilities," Lang replied.

"How long has he had a key? He could have been watching me." She shivered, and tears formed in the corner of her eyes.

"Hey, it's okay." Cameron tried to soothe her, wanting to pull her into his arms and hold her. *"CSU will figure it out."*

"Let's keep watching." Lang fast forwarded the video, watching. After over two hours, the perp left Jaden's apartment, carrying several reusable grocery bags.

"Those bags are pretty full. Besides the underwear, what else do you think the perp took?" he asked his partner.

She shook her head. *"Nothing I can think of. Nothing looks out of place. I wasn't having the best night last night."* She exchanged a pointed stare with him. *"So, I wasn't really paying attention."*

"Has anything ever looked out of place?" Lang asked, ignoring Jaden's last comment.

"*I don't think so. I've come home after a long day and found I left a light on I was sure I'd turned off or something, but nothing super obvious.*" She paused, thinking. "*Have CSU check the book shelf closest to my bedroom.*"

"Why?" Lang asked.

He waved the nearest CSU tech over. "Check the bookshelf next to the bedroom." He knew Jaden well enough that when she gave an order, he should follow it.

Once the techs swarmed the bookshelf, Jaden explained, "*My favorite series magically switched spots on me around Christmas last year. Paul and some of his family were here for the holidays. I just assumed he did it.*"

The techs took care, removing volume after volume from the shelf, and at last found something.

"Here, ma'am." The tech brought a book over then flipped it open, revealing a small video camera. "Looks like someone set up a complex video system."

"*Oh, my God,*" Jaden whispered. "*Oh, my God.*"

This time, he pulled his partner into his arms, hugging her close. "*It's okay, darling. I promise it will be okay.*"

She sniffled in his arms and clung to him. His body responded to having her so close, and he pushed the thought away. She needed to choose to go there again, not him.

Lang broke them apart. "Jaden, I know this is tough, but I need you to focus, okay?"

Jaden pulled away from him, nodding and wiping her eyes with her sleeve. "*Okay.*"

"We know how the perp got in. The video feed means he's been stalking you for a while. With it, he would know your routine, your usual comings and goings. The killings could have been planned for a while, or something new could have set him off."

Lang scrutinized Cameron but refrained from making a comment. Christ, their once-off thing that "didn't happen," as Jaden requested, had already made the rounds through the department. At least they weren't getting hauled in front of Chief

Novak to explain why they broke every rule regarding fraternization between partners.

"This perp isn't taking risks. He didn't break down the door, so changing the locks should prevent him from getting in again." He glanced at Jaden. His words didn't appear to reassure her.

"*I don't care if you change every lock in the building, I'm not staying here,*" she said, giving an involuntary shiver. "*There still is the little matter of the security system. How did he bypass that*"

"We're working on it," Lang replied. "Look, why don't you go to Cameron's place, relax a little. I'll call you as soon as we have anything."

The scowl Jaden gave Lang could have frozen the Sahara desert. "*I'll stay.*"

Lang shot him a pleading look. As much as he hated to admit it, it would do more harm than good for her to be here at this point.

"Come on, Jay. Let's go to my place. We need to finish some paperwork on Marissa's case anyway."

Jaden wavered but then caved, allowing Cameron to drive them to his condo along with a bag of her things. She would stay there until this investigation was over.

Chapter Thirteen

*J*aden sat at the dining room table, her head in her hands, staring at her laptop.

"*What's wrong?*" he asked.

They'd finished the paperwork about an ago hour and sent it off to IA. He'd spoken with Muller on the phone, explaining their current situation with as little detail as possible. He promised to smooth any bumps over with IA and for them to get together outside of work.

"*Nothing.*" She hit her keyboard hard.

"*Easy, darling.*" He walked to her and took the laptop away. "*What are you trying to do?*"

"*I can't reach Paul.*" She stared at him. Seeming lost. "*I don't know what to do.*"

"*I'm sure you'll reach him. Why don't you do something else for a while?*"

"*Like what?*"

"*I don't know. Why we don't watch some TV?*"

She scanned the big flat-screen TV and sound system dominating the space in his living room and shook her head. "*I don't feel like it.*"

"*Come on, Jay. You can't just sit here and stress. Is there something you like to do to unwind and relax?*" He shut her laptop, and she wrinkled her nose. "*Anything?*"

Jaden glanced over to the TV again. "*I like to dance.*" She blushed.

"*Then let's dance.*" He turned on his sound system, fiddling with the knobs until a slow jazz classic filled the air.

She gave him a stubborn stare when he offered her a hand. "*Really?*"

"*Come on. I'm trying to be all smooth and debonair. May I have this dance, milady?*" He resisted smirking.

She took his hand. He pulled her to her feet, spinning her into his arms.

"*That was so cheesy.*" She grinned.

"*I made you smile,*" Cameron teased. He pulled her in close and swayed with her to the music.

"*Can you turn the bass up?*"

He grabbed the remote and increased the bass until he the deep thrum vibrated in his chest. His neighbors would hate him, but the pleasure on Jaden's face made it so it didn't matter.

Some of the stress seemed to drain from her body.

"*Do you mean to do that?*" He had the bass too loud to comfortably talk over, but they could talk in the space of their minds.

"*Do what?*"

"*Send me feelings. Sometimes I get these feelings from you. Like right now you're telling me you're relaxing.*"

She shook her head. "*I don't even know I'm doing it. I shouldn't be. I'm usually good at blocking people out.*"

"*Darling, I'm not most people*"

"*Paul thinks you might be my mate.*" She frowned. "*I'm not sure I believe in that.*"

"*Would you prefer true love?*"

Jaden shook her head again. "*In a world of almost seven billion people, how can there be one person who you're supposed to spend the rest of your life with?*"

"*I don't know.*" The song changed to something faster, and he picked up the steps a bit. "*I can't answer that.*"

She stopped moving. "*Why did you sleep with Paul?*"

"*Because it felt right, Jay.*" He reached out, tilting her chin upward, forcing her to look him in the eye. "*I've always been attracted to both men and women. After what Paul told me, everything in my life finally made sense.*"

"*What did he tell you, Cameron?*"

"*He told me life wasn't fair, and I had to choose between being with you and being with him.*" He wished he could do her trick of sharing thoughts or images or memories with her. It would make explaining thing so much easier. "*He wanted me to choose you.*"

"*You slept with him,*" she pointed out, sounding a tiny bit hurt. The song changed again, another slow tune, and he pulled her close again.

"*I slept with you, too. But why can't I have both, Jay? Call me greedy, but I want you and him. I decided a long time ago I would have relationships with women and sex with men. I tried for a long time, but I was unhappy no matter what I did.*"

His eyes were closed, and he moved around the space of his apartment by memory. Almost as though this conversation was taking place in a detached realm from their physical bodies.

"*You deserve to be happy, Cam.*"

"*Don't you?*"

She stopped moving, and Jaden let go of his hands. Instead, her palms pressed to his chest, sliding upward until she reached his shoulders. Cameron lowered his head until she connected their lips. It was the first time she had started a kiss in the waking world. He waited, letting her control the pace, and when he couldn't take it anymore, he gripped her arms and leaned into her. He forced her mouth open and kissed her until she gasped for breath.

He opened his eyes, staring down into her bright-green ones. "*You make me happy.*"

"*You make me happy, too.*" She leaned in close, her stomach brushing against his groin. She raised an eyebrow at him. "*More than happy.*"

She blushed. "*Oh.*"

"*Tell me what you want, Jay.*"

He didn't want to push her, but he needed her—any part of her.

"*You won't push me into anything.*"

Damn, she read his mind. He brought his block high enough so she couldn't read his thoughts.

"Then what do you want?" His voice dropped a notch or two as he forced himself to relax—last time, things happened on his terms. This time Jaden had to be in charge.

"*I don't know.*" She trembled beneath his touch. "*You. I want you to make me feel safe again.*"

"*I'm not sure how.*"

Tears threatened to spill from her eyes. "*Try. Please? I need someone to make me feel safe. I can't find Paul, and he's....*" She shook her head.

"*He's your safe zone.*" He suddenly understood so much more.

"*You make me feel safe, too.*"

He could feel all of the conflicting emotions boiling through her. She was scared and feeling alone, but at the same time, her heart raced beneath his fingertips.

He brushed her hair out of her face. "I'll try."

They kissed again, Cameron taking his time to explore her body, to absorb her taste, her flavor. He wanted to feel every part of her and revel in it. His hands threaded through her hair.

"*Let's move this to the bedroom.*" She sighed before he kissed her again.

"*Darling, you're driving me crazy,*" Cameron said, once they broke apart.

She smirked. "*Good.*"

She grabbed the waistband of his dress pants and walked backward, pulling him toward the bedroom. He turned the music down to a more tolerable level, allowing her to guide him into his inner sanctum. He shut the door and turned her around so she pressed against it.

"You're killing me, Jay." He skimmed his fingers over her open shirt collar. She shivered beneath his touch. "Are you sure you want to do this?"

She nodded.

He could feel her—there no trace of hesitancy, nothing of fear. "Because you'll break my heart if you call this a mistake again, sweetheart."

"It's not a mistake, Cameron. It's not a mistake this time and wasn't a mistake before."

His heart pounded so loudly in his head, he could barely hear her.

He kissed her again, harder this time, more demanding. Opening herself to him, she allowed her feelings to flow. She almost overwhelmed him with her wants and desires, mixing his feelings with hers.

Grateful the maid had been there today and the sheets were clean and fresh, he led her to his bed.

He tossed off his shirt and undid Jaden's, sliding it from her shoulders. Her breasts were perfectly encased in one of her designer numbers. *Beautiful.* When he lowered his head and nipped at the hard nub through the soft, lacy material, Jaden gasped, her fingers threading through his short hair.

His hands slid around her back, undoing her bra clasp. He pulled away the material, and she squirmed under his gaze. He moved lower, his fingers brushing over her flat stomach. He kissed a spot just above the button of her jeans that made her giggle.

He unzipped her pants and pulled them away, leaving a sexy pair of panties. Lowering his mouth, he sucked on her through the soft material, and she moaned.

"Please."

He pulled the scrap of lace and silk away—then his mouth covered her. She gasped as his tongue worked over her clit, jabbing and running teasing circles around it. The hold she had on his hair tightened.

"Okay. Okay." Her fist pounded on the bed. *"Please."*

"Please what?" He gazed up at her.

"I need you. So bad."

Cameron chuckled. He pressed a kiss to her inner thigh. "I'll be right back." Standing, he undid his pants and pulled them and his boxer briefs off. He sauntered to the dresser, naked, and pulled out lube and a couple of condoms.

He dropped them on the bed next to Jaden, but she stopped him from re-joining her. She moved to the edge of the mattress and stared at him with a devious smile, before taking him into her mouth.

He gasped, and his hands found her short hair. Just holding, not guiding or forcing. "Darling, you don't have to."

As she rolled the foreskin in her mouth, moving it over the sensitive head, he groaned.

"I want to." Her soft touch on his hips as she worked him over in her mouth drove him crazy.

"God, I need you, Jay"," he said his voice deeper than usual and filled with need.

She pulled away, blushing, and he joined her on the bed. His body covered hers.

"I need you, too." Jaden pulled him down on top of her.

He paused, grabbing the condom and tearing the packet open with his teeth. Then he kissed her as he rolled it onto himself. He fumbled with the lube but still managed to coat the rubber sheath one-handed.

As he slid inside her, she cried out and arched against him.

"Okay?" He petted her hair, not moving.

She blushed. *"Sore."*

Cameron felt a tiny bit guilty. He'd forgotten she still might be sensitive after the other day. "Am I hurting you?"

She shook her head. Her hands ran down his back to squeeze his ass.

"It's taking all of my willpower not to fuck you into the mattress right now, Jay."

"Who said I wanted your willpower?" She raised her hips meeting his. *"I want you."*

He moved, slow, controlled, and steady at first. Then long strokes when a soft whimper sounded from her throat every time he slid forward, hitting that spot deep inside her. She rolled her hips to meet him, thrust for thrust. She didn't bother to ask for more, she demanded it, setting their pace and tone. He could already feel his orgasm building, but he pushed it aside. Cam needed her to come first.

He pulled away so he could kneel, pulling her legs up to his shoulders. He gazed down at her as he pumped into her in a steady rhythm. It looked so perfect, his thick cock sliding inside her. He reached down, rubbing her sensitive clit.

She moaned, long and low, from the very back of her throat. She arched against him, and he rubbed harder. As her orgasm washed over her, she tightened around him, all but screaming as she came.

Seeing her in the throes of ecstasy pushed Cameron over the edge, and he cried out her name as he pumped into her the last few times, before collapsing forward and landing on his elbows so he didn't crush her.

She pulled him down on top of her, so his full weight rested on her body. His mouth found hers, and they kissed, both gasping for breath.

"*That was even better than the last time.*" Jay whispered her voice sounding far away.

"*It was.*"

He kissed her once more before he slid out of her. He sighed as he did so. He rolled over, and she cuddled into him, resting her head on his shoulder.

Jaden stayed, and it wasn't long before he realized she had fallen asleep. He kissed her and climbed out of bed. He went to the bathroom and got rid of the condom. Then he wandered naked through the condo, shutting it down for the night.

He slipped into bed, tucking the covers around himself and Jaden. "Night," he whispered to her, kissing her hair.

"*Night, Cam,*" she mumbled mentally. Half-asleep, she snuggled into him, and he fell asleep holding her close.

Chapter Fourteen

Cameron sat at his desk, nursing a headache. Jaden had been raging since they woke to the news of a fifth murder. Same MO and another pair of her underwear found at the scene. With the words "I'm watching you, Black" written in the victim's blood on the bedroom wall. When she raged like this, he felt the pain. The knot in his stomach grew with every victim they found, every threat.

He swallowed a couple Tylenols Ruth gave him, hoping to at least dull the ache. He clicked through still photos of the perp, trying to catch a glimpse of his face. The only part he had seen clearly so far was the man's forehead. Whoever he was, he'd done enough pre-scouting he knew where the cameras were and how to avoid them.

Lang entered the small room that Special Investigations called home and stalked over to him.

"We've got a problem." She seemed exhausted, her hair coming out in every which way, as though she had run her fingers through it a million times.

"What kind of problem?" His head pounded harder. He didn't think he could take one more setback on this case.

He motioned for her to sit in the chair next to his desk. She did.

"The media got a hold of it. They've already given him a nickname."

He swore. The media complicated everything. They had a nasty habit of blowing everything out of proportion—or worse—minimizing things when they were serious. Thankfully, their unit was kept under wraps as much as possible, getting minimal to no media exposure.

"What do they know?"

"They're reporting four murders in a row with the same MO, and that the woman is identical, or made up to appear identical, to a female detective in the Toronto PD. They don't have the details about which detective, the underwear, or the DNA. Thank God."

"Still, that's an awful lot to know. Think we have a leak in the department?" Cameron's first concern was for Jaden's safety. If someone was leaking information to the media, they could put her at risk by leaking her location. When she was in the office, it was fine—dozens of armed detective were a few feet away. But when they were home, it was just Cameron—and he had developed a nasty habit of letting his guard down when she was around.

"Maybe. A lot can be picked up by police scanners, though. There might be someone just confirming, but I couldn't even begin to guess whom. We've got half a dozen detectives working the case, plus God knows how many admin assistants and CSU personnel."

"Needle in a bloody haystack."

Lang nodded.

"What nickname did the media give him anyway?" He rolled through possible names in his head, but nothing seemed to fit—much like the rest of this case.

Lang shook her head in disgust. "It's bad. They're calling him the Look-Alike Killer. Women with black hair everywhere are freaking out and buying bleach."

Cameron shared her dismay. This was bad. "Well, at least they don't know the perp dyed the second victim's hair black before he cut it."

"True. Still, how can we issue a broad warning? 'If you think you look like this police officer, please use extra caution, as a crazy murderer is out to get you.' The chief would have my head if I put something like that out there, inciting public panic and all that. Plus, according to HQ, Jaden is just a publicity stunt for female policing."

"What!" Cameron shouted.

"Relax, will you? Official word is Jaden's special...talents don't exist. They need a cover for her being so young. The unofficial word is we had better protect the best asset this police force has. They're trying to guard her, and themselves, against a media storm if word of Jaden's...special abilities got out."

"I hate the media."

"Sorry to interrupt, kids." Ruth stuck her head around the corner of the cubicle. "You're going to want to see this."

He exchanged a glare with Lang and stood up, walking the two feet over to Ruth's desk.

"Here." She turned the volume on the speakers and pressed "play" on the video feed.

A female reporter with dark-brown hair appeared on screen in front of the latest crime scene. "We have just gotten word from a confidential police informant that the detective who is being targeted in these crimes is Detective Jaden Black from the Special Investigations Unit. Detective Black is one of the youngest members of the Toronto Police Department and is the youngest detective in the history of the police force. Sources say the murdered women are similar in appearance to Detective Black, seen here in this undated photo."

A photo of Jaden popped up on the screen. In the picture, she sat on a bench, laughing, the beach in the background. She appeared younger, tanned, and relaxed. He had never seen the photo before. Where the hell had it come from?

"We are urging women who are similar in appearance to take extra steps regarding their safety tonight as we wait to see if the Look-Alike Killer will strike for a third night in a row and sixth time in recent months. Our calls to Toronto Police have not been returned."

The feed cut off.

"Fuck me in the ass," Ruth said.

He nodded. "You can say that again."

Lang pinched the bridge of her nose. "How the hell did they get the information? We haven't even officially connected the other three murders yet."

"Not sure. Right now the report is just on the Internet, but it will hit the five o'clock news in two hours. Two hours to quash it as much as possible. Want me to call the chief's office?" Ruth asked.

"And Media Relations," Lang added. "Let's see if we can change the tone of the report a little bit."

"On it."

Ruth picked up the phone, and Lang left the office chatting on her mobile, making calls. His phone vibrated, and he pulled it out. A text message from an unknown number.

Coffee shop around the corner, twenty minutes, come alone. Logan.

He stood up and scanned over the cubicles. Jaden had curled into her chair, eyes closed. She frowned as if she was still trying to reach Paul. She hadn't heard from him since she told him what had been going on, early yesterday.

"Ruth," he murmured, as she was on the phone. She nodded in acknowledgment. "I need to run out for a few minutes. Make sure Jaden doesn't go anywhere, okay?"

She nodded again.

"Thanks."

He stood and grabbed his suit jacket, shrugging it on. He left their little room and made his way through Homicide. No one shot a second glance at him as he hit the down button on the elevator.

Letting out a sigh of relief, he left the building. He blocked against Jaden's intruding thoughts. Whatever Logan wanted to tell him, he wasn't sure Jaden should hear it. He walked the two blocks to the coffee shop, crowded, but he spotted Logan and his partner, Chris Muller, in the far corner. Logan held up a cup, indicating they had already gotten him a coffee.

He moved past the lineup and joined them at the back of the room.

"Large black coffee, right?" Chris asked when he reached them.

"Perfect, thanks." He accepted the take-out cup and took the top off, blowing on the still steaming liquid. He waited for one of them to say something.

"You're probably wondering why we brought you out here all cloak and dagger style," Logan said at last.

He made a noise of encouragement. Silence is a great tool for getting people to talk.

"We saw the news report about Jaden being the detective who the Look-Alike Killer is targeting."

He nodded.

"The photo the newscast used. It's on her computer."

"How could you know that?"

"I saw it the other day when I was going through the stuff you had on Meincke." Logan glanced at Chris who nodded for him to continue. "I'm a technopath. I can control technology with my mind. When I touch a computer, I see everything. The files, the folders, the pictures, the documents. I automatically index everything into my head. I have an eidetic memory."

"What's that?"

Logan rolled his eyes, so Chris answered. "Better known as a photographic memory. Logan can see and process information on computers at an alarming rate. He also stores it away for future use."

"He keeps thinking I should go on *Jeopardy*," Logan added.

"Next Ken Jennings," Chris bantered.

"Right, anyway." Cameron refocused them. "You saw the photo on Jaden's computer, and...?"

"I think someone installed a phishing software program on there. It's been on there a while—from the time the computer was activated almost. At first, I thought it was something Jaden had done. An auto backup onto a desktop or secondary drive in case her laptop crashed. Now I'm thinking someone else installed it to spy on her." Logan took a sip of his coffee, waiting for Cam to process the information.

Dammit. Jaden knew there was something different about Logan. Telepaths had a sixth sense around each other. "You're coming to this conclusion based on a piece of software you think someone installed on her laptop." The idea of Logan being a technopath wasn't totally foreign to him. There was one on reality TV who could make mass text messages appear and scramble phone or GPS signals. The fact the department had one and this was the first he'd heard about it did surprise him. He did, however, struggle to see how Logan could know everything he had just told him.

"Jaden's computer has been outfitted with department software. It's not the easiest thing to break into and bypass." Logan seemed frustrated Cameron hadn't made the same connection he had. "It's not impossible, but whoever did this had advanced knowledge of computers and has been keeping an eye on Jaden for an extended period of time."

Right, someone had been stalking Jaden for a while. They'd already guessed that based on the fact the perp had installed surveillance in her apartment. He knew her patterns, her comings and goings. Almost everything about her. More, it appeared, than even Cam knew about her.

"Can you trace the software to whoever installed it?"

"I can," Logan replied.

"But?"

"I can't actually insert myself into this investigation," he explained. "Unless it's a child sex crimes case, I'm hands-off."

"Or IA," Chris added.

"So, we do this off the books, then." Cameron paused as a dark-haired woman passed them, making her way to the bathroom.

Chris shook his head. "It's not that simple. If Logan does get anything off the computer, it can't be used in court, or even officially in the investigation."

"So, we're having this meeting because?"

"We need to find a way for Lang to trigger an IA investigation. We need to do it in such a way that she doesn't suspect we're playing her. Lang's straight by the book. Anything looks off and she won't be happy."

"Well, triggering an investigation should be easy. Lang already suspects someone is leaking information to the media."

"Here's the tricky part." Logan and Chris exchanged glances. "We want her to set up an investigation into you."

"Me?" Cameron said, a little louder than necessary. A few people gave a cursory glance their way, but when it was clear they were not going to say anything of interest they went back to their coffees. "Why me?"

"Because we know you're clean," Chris replied. "We already did the work on you. So that way, we can focus on Jaden and not the fake investigation."

Cameron shook his head. He took a long swallow of his coffee which had cooled sufficiently since their conversation started. "How do you suggest I do such a thing?"

Logan smiled. "It's easy. Just have Ruth suggest to Lang that you're the one leaking information. Have her mention IA. As soon as the report comes in, we'll do the rest."

"So, Ruth can be in on this?"

They nodded.

"What about Jaden?"

Chris blew out a breath. "We want to wait to tell her. Most likely the person who got this software installed on the computer didn't do it remotely."

"You're suggesting whoever is threatening Jaden is close to her?"

They both nodded.

"Very close," Logan added. "She must have willingly handed her computer over to whoever installed it. It would have triggered too many safeties otherwise. Alarms would have gone off if they had tried to hack it."

He rubbed his hands over his face. He had only borrowed her laptop a handful of times since she got it. He knew Ruth had borrowed it. Other than police techs who'd worked on it, no one else had access to it as far as he was aware.

"You realize that narrows it down to me, Ruth, and police techs, right?"

"We know," Logan replied.

He blew out a big breath.

"Okay, I'll call Ruth and see what we can do to get Lang to trigger the investigation." He dialed her number.

"Where have you gotten off to?" she asked, by way of answering the phone.

"Is Jaden around?"

"Mmhmm, in her chair. Need me to ask her something?"

"Opposite."

"Right. What's up?"

"I'm meeting with Weber and Muller," he stated.

"Uh-huh."

"They want in on the investigation. Logan thinks he found something on Jaden's computer, but to use it in the investigation they need to be invited in."

"Uh-huh," she prompted.

"They need you to tell Lang that you think I'm the one leaking information to the media and suggest she call IA. They'll handle the rest."

Ruth sighed. "Do you have any idea how hard that is to do? She won't go running to IA for nothing."

"You need to convince her it's not nothing, Ruth. It's for Jaden."

"You know I can't say no when it comes to Jaden. I'll see what I can do. No promises." She disconnected.

"Thank you," Logan said when he set the phone down. "I know it's not easy, but once we are officially brought in, I should be able to trace where the information the software collects is being sent to."

"Hopefully, it will lead us to the killer," Chris added then took a sip of coffee.

The woman who had gone to the bathroom came out, and they were silent as she passed.

Cameron glanced at his watch—after five. "We need to wrap this up. Once Lang is done dealing with the media, Ruth should be able to convince her to get the ball rolling on the investigation."

"For sure if we get called in tonight, I'll send you a text. Maybe I can get my hands on Jaden's computer," Logan said, and stood.

Cameron and Chris followed. They shook hands outside of the coffee shop before each going their separate ways.

Lang appeared annoyed when he returned to the office.

"Where have you been?" Her eyes narrowed.

"Just out at a meeting. How did working with Media Relations go?"

Lang scowled. "Fine. I've managed to put a nicer spin on it. Warning all women, especially those who live alone, to be vigilant, rather than just those who look like Jaden. I'm sure the six o'clock news will have the press conference headlining."

He glanced at one of the many clocks on the wall, almost five-thirty. "I'll check back around six."

He made his way to the little room where Jaden still sat in her chair and Ruth worked away on her computer.

"Raking in the overtime, Ruth?" She was usually gone by five.

She made a noise. "Spoke with Chief Novak's assistant. He's throwing everything he can at this. Having someone murder people because they look like a cop isn't sitting very well with him."

"Of course. How's Jaden?"

"Hasn't moved from her chair since you left. I would almost say she was asleep, but once in a while she'll type something on her laptop."

"Did you talk to Lang?"

She made a noise in the back of her throat.

"And?"

"We'll see. I did my best." Her phone rang. "Special Investigations, can I help you?"

She waved her hand at him. Point taken, he could go.

He returned to his desk, feeling at a loss for what to do. He had no leads to run down, no one to call. Everything Logan and Chris had given him pointed not to a stalker but someone privy to parts of Jaden even he didn't know.

"You shouldn't think so hard."

He startled at her voice, not expecting her to be able to talk to him through his block. *"Sorry?"*

"I can tell you're fretting about something. Even if I'm not sure exactly what you're worried about."

"You."

"I'm fine."

"I can still worry."

"You can."

The door to Special Investigations burst opened.

"We've got him," Lang said.

"Who?" He felt stupid as soon as he said it.

"The perp." She rolled her eyes. "Patrol arrested him after he entered Jaden's apartment using a key. We've had them sitting inside in case he decided to come back."

"Really?"

"Really. Patrol is transporting him here now. He should be arriving any minute."

Jaden blew out a loud sigh of relief. *"Oh, thank God."* She sank further into her chair.

He nodded in agreement. Lang left to meet them downstairs. Cameron sat at his desk, eager to get a shot at whoever had killed those five women and terrorized Jaden. Something ate away at him, though. It seemed almost too easy for the perp to get caught walking into Jaden's place. He was smart, very smart according to Logan and Chris. To walk into a trap seemed a little unlikely.

Maybe he was thinking too hard on this. Tension left Jaden's face at the news. His phone vibrated with a text from Lang saying she was on her way with the suspect.

"*I want to see him. I need to see him.*"

"All right, but stay back."

He took her by the arm and escorted her to the elevators. They stood behind the glass door that had the Toronto PD Homicide crest on it, the frosted emblem obscuring them from sight. He placed himself protectively in front of her.

The doors to the elevators slid open, and Jaden let out an audible gasp.

"*Paul!*"

Chapter Fifteen

*C*ameron's reactions seemed slow as Jaden pushed him out of the way.

"*Paul!*" she screamed. She ran out into the hallway.

Everyone in the area paused. A few even covered their ears in an attempt to block her out, not knowing where the noise had come from.

"*What the hell, Lang? Release him this instant!*"

"Jaden," Lang said.

"*Keys!*" She held out her hand.

Everyone in the area had stopped to watch the interaction. Lang shook her head. Jaden went to Cameron who had joined them in the hallway in front of the elevators. She reached into his pocket and pulled out the key ring, which included a handcuff key. She unlocked Paul's cuffs.

He rubbed his wrists. "Thanks, luv. I was trying to tell them I owned the place, but they wouldn't listen."

"*What the hell are you doing here?*" She projected her thoughts so he and Lang could participate in the conversation. "*You should be in Australia.*"

"When you told me what was happening, I took the first flight I could here. I've been on planes or in airports for the last twenty-five or so hours."

"You have proof of this?" Lang eyed him.

"As I tried to tell your bobbies, my plane tickets and passport with entry stamp were in the briefcase they confiscated at Jaden's flat." Paul's accent exaggerated at the word bobbies. "Proof I've just arrived from Australia is in there."

"He couldn't have committed any murders." Jaden clicked her teeth and turned to the people who were still watching them. *"Get back to work. Show's over."*

All of the sudden, everyone else had somewhere else to be, and they scampered away.

Lang gave Paul a once over. "I apologize for the misunderstanding. I still have some questions for you if you wouldn't mind."

"Of course." Paul turned toward Jaden. "As soon as I finish with Detective Lang here, why don't we go out and have a nice dinner? Take our minds off all of this unpleasantness, luv."

She nodded. *"We'll be in Special Investigations."* Jaden shot daggers at Lang with her eyes. *"Just drop him off there when you're done."*

"Of course." Lang showed Paul to one of the interview rooms.

"Come on, Jay," Cam said. *"Let's not make any more of a scene."*

Jaden clicked her teeth but allowed him to show her into their tiny inner sanctum.

"I can't believe them. Arresting Paul."

He closed the door to their offices.

"How could they?"

"Think how it looks, Jay. You tell them Paul is in Australia, they know the perp has a key. Him showing up and letting himself into your place, they made a natural assumption."

"Assume makes an ass out of you and me," Jaden zinged.

"Agreed."

It didn't take long for Lang to finish questioning Paul and bring him to their tiny corner of the world.

"Sorry for all of the trouble." Lang shook the older man's

hand. "I've arranged for them to bring your luggage here rather than being logged into evidence."

"Thank you very much, Rhonda," Paul said.

Cameron exchanged a thought with his partner. *Rhonda?*

"I'm sure I'll see you soon." Rhonda replied then excused herself.

The second she disappeared from the doorway, Jaden launched herself into Paul's arms. *"You're here."*

"Of course I'm here, luv. When you told me about the first girl, I couldn't stay away." He rocked her as he hugged her.

"Thank you."

"Come on, then. As soon as my luggage gets here, why don't we head out? Dinner for all of us, my treat."

He brushed Jaden's hair out of her face, causing her to wrinkle her nose in the way Cam found adorable.

"Sure. That sounds great."

Paul stared over Jaden to Cameron and winked. "How are you doing?"

Cameron felt himself blush. His body reacted to the older man, but despite having slept with him in Dreamworld, Cameron realized he knew almost nothing about the guy. A common problem he'd started to find annoying about his life. "I'm alright, thanks."

A knock sounded at the door, followed by a patrol officer sticking his head into their tiny room. "We have some luggage sent to evidence by mistake."

"That would be mine." Paul let go of Jaden and collected the briefcase, small wheeled bag, and much larger suitcase. "Thank you very much for returning it."

"No problem, sir. Detectives." The officer disappeared.

Ruth came over, carrying a few file folders. "Why don't you kids head out? I'm almost done for the day. I just have to give these files to Lang."

"It would be a pleasure if the famous Ruth would join us." Paul's blue eyes sparkled at her.

Ruth blushed and laughed, swatting at him. "Maybe another

time. You go have fun." She hurried out of the room.

"How do you know Ruth?" Cameron asked.

"Oh, I met her when Jaden first started working with the department," Paul replied. "Shall we?"

He led them to the elevators. A few curious glances got shot their way, but no one said anything, thankfully. They went out through Security—who had a fit with Paul because he hadn't been properly checked into the building—then down to the garage.

Jaden climbed into the driver's seat while Cameron and Paul loaded his bags into the trunk.

"Cameron," Paul said, shutting the hatchback with a small slam. "I know you must have a lot of questions."

"That's putting it mildly."

"I promise tonight I'll answer everything, but for the moment we need to focus on Jaden." Paul glanced through the tinted glass at her. "She needs all the support she can get."

"Agreed."

The older man climbed into the front seat, and Cameron took the rear. Jaden drove, heading out of the garage toward a trendy downtown restaurant.

They kept the conversation at dinner light, away from the topics looming over them. Paul spent a lot of time talking about the wildlife rescue he ran in Australia and about a particular platypus he was worried about. After dinner, they headed to Cameron's condo. Paul tried to say he would stay in a hotel, but Jaden insisted he stay with them, with Cameron's permission.

When they got in, Jaden headed straight to bed, curling up with David in the spare room. It seemed she had figured what was coming next.

Paul settled on the couch with Cameron and two beers. The older man sipped his beer, regarding him. "So, what do you want to know?"

"Everything," Cameron replied, almost too fast. "I thought I knew Jaden really well. It turns out I had barely scratched the surface. I want to know everything about you, about her."

Paul smiled. "Ask anything."

His accent seemed thicker than it had at first, indicating he might be tired after a day of travel and the emotional turmoil of the past few hours.

"What kind of accent do you have?"

Paul laughed low and soft, sounding even sexier than he had in Dreamworld. "I don't have an accent. You do." He paused for a moment before continuing. "I was born in Ireland, lived there until I was five then moved to London. When I was twenty, I lived in the U.S. for five years then Canada for another five, before I finally settled in Australia."

"Why all the moving around?"

"Ireland was in economic decline, my aunt lost her job. She eventually found one in London, so we moved there. After Adeline died, I couldn't stand to stay in London, so as soon as I could, I moved to the U.S. I finished my schooling there and got my master's degree. Then I came to Canada to support Jaden. She was seven at the time. That's when her parents died." Paul polished off his beer. "Want another?"

Cameron shook his head. "I'm fine."

Paul went to the kitchen and returned with another beer.

"Jaden's parents died?" Cameron felt floored. She had never mentioned her parents, but he'd had no clue they were dead.

"When she was seven."

"How?"

Paul shrugged, indicating he didn't know, or he knew and wouldn't tell him. "She was in foster care until she became an emancipated minor at sixteen. She finished high school at twelve, got her first degree at fourteen, and finished her masters at seventeen and law degree while at the Academy. Joined the force the day after she turned eighteen."

"I didn't know any of that." Cameron took a long swallow of his beer. "I knew she had a couple of university degrees. I don't even know what they're in."

"Most people don't. She has a bachelor's of criminology and Socio-Legal Studies with a master's in Legal Theory. Black isn't her original last name either. It's the name of the woman who was her foster mom for almost ten years. She changed it when she turned sixteen. They are still very close."

"There is a lot about her I don't know." He felt a little left out, having to learn this from Paul rather than Jaden. He'd never had any clues as to her past.

Paul reached over and squeezed Cameron's shoulder. "Don't feel bad, mate. She doesn't talk about her childhood much. It was very difficult for her. Try being able to read everyone's minds at the age of two."

"I never thought of it like that," he admitted. "I just see her as she is now."

"I only see her that way because I saw her going through it," Paul replied. "If I met her now, I would never guess what she's been through over the years."

"It's still amazing you've known her since she was three," Cameron told him. "I can't even imagine what she looked like at that age."

"She had long black hair that she never let her mum brush, and she always had a skinned knee or a bruise or ten. I remember once when she was six, she broke her arm falling out of a tree."

"Ouch," Cameron replied. "How did she manage to fall out of a tree?"

"Fell climbing up, caught herself halfway down on the swing, and caused a spiral fracture of her arm. Triggered a CPS investigation." Paul laughed and shook his head. "Jaden had the investigators running in circles looking all over the place for the fun of it. They figured out pretty fast she was playing them, but she had fun while it lasted."

"Sounds like Jaden. Ultimate control freak." Cameron laughed.

"Even at six."

Cameron polished off his beer and set the bottle on the table. He went to settle on the couch, but Paul stopped him. He leaned into him and kissed him instead. Paul tasted like beer and something else that left him wanting more.

The older man pulled away, with a soft smile. "I didn't fly

here for this, you know."

"I know. Jaden would have called you out in a second if you had."

Paul chuckled, the sound reverberating deep from his chest.

"You're right, but since I'm here...." He shrugged.

Cameron gripped his lover's dress shirt and pulled him in close, their lips meeting for second time. This kiss was harder, more demanding. Paul's hand moved over Cameron's chest, his fingers undoing the buttons of his shirt. They slid inside, ghosting over his nipples and traveling lower.

Cameron's hands mirrored Paul's actions, unbuttoning his dress shirt and pulling it out of his pants, his fingers working on his lover's belt.

"How far did you want to go?" The older man pulled away from their kiss.

His hands stilled. "I'm not sure." He felt nervous. Paul had pushed for him to bottom before, and he honestly wasn't ready for that in the real world.

Paul kissed him again, softer this time. "We'll go at your pace."

"Thank you," Cameron murmured, kissing him again. He finished undoing his lover's belt and dress pants, sliding a hand inside to palm his thick cock. Paul let out a healthy moan, his fingers working on Cameron's belt.

He groaned in turn as Paul's hand slid inside his pants, then growled as Paul's fingers pinched and rolled his foreskin.

"You're uncut, and you're thick." Paul grinned.

"Of course I am. You saw me in Dreamworld."

"Sometimes what we see in Dreamworld doesn't always translate to the real world," he explained. "I'm glad it did this time."

He disentangled his hand from Paul's pants and pulled him in for another kiss.

"Why don't we move this to the bedroom?"

A soft noise sounded from the back of Paul's throat. He gave one last cursory tug to Cameron's hard cock before removing his hands. "I think that's a good idea."

He stood and kissed the shorter man, pulling him into the bedroom. Their shirts hit the floor on the way, as did their pants. They fell into bed, both wearing nothing but their underwear.

He landed on top of the older man, kissing him. Paul's hands moved lower. He squeezed Cameron's ass through his boxer briefs, roughly massaging. Cam slipped a hand between them, pushed Paul's briefs down, and moved his hand to his lover's cock, gliding over the loose foreskin. His lover moaned into the kiss.

"I've never been with another guy who's uncut before. I love it." Cam groaned between kisses.

Paul's hands slid inside Cam's underwear. He dragged a finger down his crack, teasing his opening. Cameron hissed as zings of pleasure shot through his body.

"Who said I was going to bottom?" He nipped at Paul's lower lip.

"Who said I was going to?" Paul pressed a finger into Cameron, not all the way, but enough that he felt its presence.

"It appears we have a stalemate." He raised an eyebrow at Paul, challenging him.

"How about we suck each other off until we decide who wants to fuck whom?"

Cameron laughed. "Nice dirty talk."

He allowed Paul to push his boxer briefs the rest of the way off. He wiggled out of them and responded to the tug on his side. He turned around so his face lined up with Paul's cock, and Paul's mouth with his.

His lover immediately took him into his mouth, sucking. Cameron returned the favor. He moaned around Paul, as the older man swallowed him all the way to the root. Cameron worked on rolling his partner's foreskin over in his mouth, enjoying the taste. It wasn't overpowering, like other guys he had been with, but intoxicating. He drank it in, focusing on the spots that made the older man moan, enjoying the vibrations reverberating down his spine.

He swallowed Paul deep, as his lover moved lower, lavishing his sack with his tongue before moving even lower. Paul honed in on his entrance. Cameron whimpered around Paul as his lover kissed and licked over his body. He all but forgot he was supposed to be giving Paul as much pleasure as he was receiving.

A tube of lube bouncing off his head and landing next to him remedied that.

"Want to feel your fingers inside of me," Paul said, between long strokes of his tongue.

Cameron kept sucking on the other man's cock, focusing on the underside of the head and the slit on top, loving the little moans coming from the back of Paul's throat as he rimmed his ass.

He got the lube open with one hand and squished some onto his fingers. Paul widened his thighs as Cameron sought his opening. He cried out as the first digit slipped inside.

"Fuck, you're tight."

Cameron pulled off Paul's cock. His lover responded by tightening the muscles, almost painfully, around Cameron's finger. God, he couldn't wait to be inside him. Cam knew who was going to get fucked, tonight anyway.

"Give me another," Paul demanded.

Cameron complied. With two fingers inside him, he twisted upward, searching for his sweet spot. He knew he found it when Paul inhaled sharply then moaned.

Copious amounts of pre-cum drooled down the side of his lover's cock, and Cameron lapped it up. He worked a third finger in, and his lover squirmed beneath him. He had stopped rimming Cameron and just made heady moans, causing him to ache with need.

"Can I fuck you?" He took the head of older man's cock into his mouth.

"God, yes," Paul breathed. "I need you, Cam."

It took them a moment to disentangle themselves, and they laughed as he almost tumbled off the bed. Paul kissed him once Cameron had settled top of him, their bodies pressed together.

"Are you sure you want to do this?" Cameron kissed Paul again, deeply drinking, loving his flavor, and the slight hint of his own taste on his lips.

"God, yes."

Paul grabbed a condom off the nightstand and tore the packet open with his teeth. Cameron moved so Paul could roll the rubber onto him. He then added lube to the outside. The older man kissed him then Cameron pushed him down against the pillows. He pulled Paul's legs up and slid a finger inside him with ease. He twisted it, tugging gently on the outside rim. His lover growled and bucked his hips.

"Ready?" he asked, pulling his fingers away.

Paul nodded.

Cameron positioned himself and sunk into him. He met resistance almost immediately and stopped, waiting while his partner's body adjusted to him. He moved in a bit farther, repeating the process until he'd buried himself deep. Paul had lost a bit of his hard on, but his eyes were still wide with pleasure

His lover shifted his hips with a slight bounce. Cameron waited, letting him move on his own. Eventually, the friction got to him, and he gave some gentle thrusts, testing Paul's reaction. He moaned and nodded, giving him permission. They started slow but quickly built a fast pace.

He switched their position. Kneeling, he pulled Paul's feet to his shoulders, his hands taking advantage of the position to play with the older man's hardened cock. The change in position meant he hit his lover's prostate with every thrust, sending him toward climax.

Cameron could feel his own orgasm building. Paul moved his hands away from his cock, so Cameron's hands relocated to his thighs, gripping tightly, as he pounded into him, enjoying the sound his balls made when they slapped against Paul's round ass.

"I'm going to.... Urgh, yeah, that's it," Paul called out as his ass contracted around Cameron.

He increased his speed, allowing his own orgasm to start. His lover cried out as thick sticky strings shot out of his cock, coating their stomachs and chests. Cameron slammed into Paul, grunting, his body awash with pleasure.

He allowed Paul's legs to fall away and collapsed forward. They kissed, wet and sloppy, both men gasping for breath. Then he rolled off to one side, still struggling to breathe.

"Fuck me," Paul said.

"I think I just did." Cameron propped himself onto his elbow.

His lover looked gorgeous, his blond hair plastered to his head, his body sweaty and sticky from cum. He had never seen a hotter sight. He bent to capture his lover's lips again, the kiss soft and quick.

"You did. If I had the energy, I'd fuck you now."

He grinned. "Yeah, well you can't help it if you're old."

Paul smacked his chest and snuggled against the pillows. "You should go get rid of that." He nodded to the condom still hanging off his softened cock,

"Yeah, I'll be right back." Cameron kissed him and slid out of bed. He padded into the bathroom where he stripped off the condom, then used a facecloth to wash. He rinsed it out and brought it to Paul. He wiped away the sticky pools of cum and lube, and they re-dressed, Cameron in boxer briefs and Paul in PJ pants. They settled into bed, Paul resting with his head on his chest.

A soft knock at the door broke Cameron from the edge of sleep.

"Yeah," he called.

Jaden stuck her head in, dressed in a pair of low hanging PJ pants with some cartoon character and a matching tank top. She was barefoot and clutching David. *"Can I sleep with you?"* she whispered.

"Sure, luv," Paul replied. "Come here."

Paul moved over, and Cameron shifted toward the middle to make room for her. Paul didn't react to her appearance, even though she had probably heard them. Cameron wanted to try and explain their actions, but Jaden didn't seem to mind. She climbed in bed and crawled over him to lie in the middle. He moved toward the edge to give her enough space. She curled up with her back facing him, snuggling in close, hinting she wanted him to cuddle her. He rolled onto his side, spooning her. She sighed, seeming not to care they had just had sex.

Cameron let it slide, but they would eventually have to have a conversation about this. He stifled a yawn as she got comfortable. She reached out, touching Paul, whose face squashed into a pillow.

"*Thank you,*" she mumbled.

Cameron pressed a kiss to the back of her neck.

"You're welcome. Go to sleep."

"*Night.*" The word came on the edge of sleep. "*Love you,*" she whispered only to him.

Cameron felt shocked for a moment then held her a tiny bit closer. "*Love you, too.*"

He drifted into sleep, finding himself lying on top of a mound of treasure in a cave.

He was a brilliant red and covered in black spines, with a tiny black dragon tucked under his arm and a much larger green one breathing fire on them, protecting both of them. He relaxed in the knowledge that his partner and his lover were safe in Dreamworld. He slipped into sleep without a further thought.

Chapter Sixteen

"You can't come with us, Paul."

Cameron dug through his closet, half-dressed, trying to find a shirt that didn't clash with the suit he wanted to wear.

"Why not?" Paul stood behind him, already in a suit, having the air of a detective more than Jaden ever did.

Cameron grabbed a green shirt out. "You're not a cop. You're not even a consultant. If a defense attorney found out I let a civilian into a crime scene, then all of the evidence collected would be inadmissible."

Lang had phoned ten minutes before to tell him, for a third night in a row, a woman who appeared almost identical to Jaden had been murdered in her home, posed to resemble her, and wore a set of Jaden's underwear the perp had stolen from her condo.

"That shirt clashes. Go with the red one." Paul sat on the edge of the bed. "I don't care. This person is threatening Jay. I should be there to protect her."

"Paul." Cameron pulled the red shirt out then shrugged it on and turned to face his lover. "I know you want to protect her, and you do. In Dreamworld. It's my duty to protect her in the waking world. Having you at the scene—I don't mean this in a bad way—

but it's a liability. I'd have to split my attention between you and her. Right now, my full attention needs to be on her safety."

Paul didn't seem happy, but after a long pause, he let out a sigh. "You're right. You should be focusing on Jaden and catching the guy threatening her, not babysitting me."

"Thank you for understanding." Cameron buttoned his shirt and crossed the distance between them, settling for a chaste kiss before he pulled away.

"*Are you ready?*" Jaden asked from the kitchen.

"*Two minutes.*" Cameron slid on his socks and fastened his belt, securing his side arm as he stepped out of the bedroom. Already dressed, she sat at the table, pushing the eggs Paul had made around on the plate—she'd eaten maybe two bites. "*We don't have to go right now. It will probably be a while before the coroner gets there. Why don't you try to eat some more?*"

"*I'm not hungry,*" she admitted, shoving the plate away. "*I can't stop thinking this is all my fault.*"

"*How is it your fault?*" Cameron asked. "*You're not the lunatic killing them.*"

"*If it wasn't for me, they wouldn't be dead.*" Standing, she headed to the door to yank on a pair of boots.

"*Darling,*" Cameron said, following her, "*if it wasn't you he was obsessing over, it would be someone else. None of this is your fault. I promise you.*"

She shrugged on a jacket. "*Thank you. I know that's total bullshit, but it does make me feel better.*"

She opened the door to the condo and set off the alarm. Crap, he'd forgotten he'd set it. He disarmed it. His cell phone rang thirty seconds later.

He glanced at the caller ID. His security company. "Hello?"

"This is Security Tech calling," the woman said. "We received an alarm from your residence. Can you tell me your security phrase?"

Cameron sighed. "Prepare to be assimilated." He prayed Jaden wouldn't get the reference.

"Thank you, Mr. Olsen. Do you require any assistance?"

"No, we're fine, thank you. It was an accidental alarm trigger."

Jaden giggled.

"All right, thank you for choosing Security Tech. Have a nice day." The woman hung up.

Jaden burst into loud, off-key laughter. *"That is your security phrase? I had no idea you were a fan."*

"Shh...." He swatted her arm. *"Let's go."* He called into the apartment, "Paul, we're going. I'll call later and let you know what's going on."

Paul appeared from the bedroom. "Have a good day." They exchanged a glance that said so much more than words.

"We'll be fine, Paul."

Jaden followed Cameron out the door and down to the SUV. She plugged the address of the latest crime scene into the GPS and they were off. The scene was almost too close for comfort, taking them less than ten minutes to arrive at the house in heavy morning traffic.

The media swarmed the area, crowding around the SUV to see who arrived at the scene. The officer at the street barricade waved them through. A great many of the neighbors stood outside in their housecoats and PJ's, watching the circus. Something like this would rock the quiet suburb.

Lang stood outside, smoking, when they pulled in front of the house.

"You made it through the media throng." She puffed on her smoke. "They were here just after the first officer arrived. I got woken up by a media call, dispatch hadn't notified homicide yet."

"Christ," he swore. "Did it go out over the radio?"

"Nope. Same MO as last two times. Perp called it in and dispatch called it in to patrol. Nothing went over the air."

"Do you think the perp called the media?" Jaden asked. *"Maybe he's enjoying the attention?"*

Lang took one last drag of her smoke before tossing it into the street. "I think that's exactly what he did. Come on."

After donning their protective gear, they entered the house

and went upstairs to the bedroom. The scene was almost an exact copy of the first two. The woman bled out from a series of cuts, most likely made by a single-edge blade. First strikes to minor arteries then to major ones, finishing with a coup de grace across the neck. He then cleaned the body and posed her—Just liked the last two victims. He'd also raped the women—the jury was still out as to whether it was before or after he killed them, or both.

"Fuck," Cameron shook his head at the sight in front of him.

The scene was even worse than the last. The words "You're next, Black" had been scrawled on the wall in what looked like the victim's blood.

Jaden blanched, losing some of her usual composure.

"*Well,*" she said after a time, "*at least there won't be any more innocent victims.*"

"We're going to catch this guy, Jaden," Lang replied. "In the meantime, I'll see if we can get authorization for an additional officer to be assigned to you."

Jaden shook her head. "*Cameron is fine.*"

"*Darling,*" he said, only to her, "*an extra officer to keep his eye on you wouldn't be such a bad idea. It would free me up to do other things.*"

She glanced between Cameron and Lang. "*Fine, but I want a uniform, not some detective who is going to try and boss me around.*"

"Have anyone in mind?" Lang asked.

"McKenzie, Third Precinct, second rotation," Cameron replied. The kid who'd watched Jaden for him when he met with Judge Silva. He seemed solid and reliable.

Lang shrugged. "I'll see what I can do."

She went to make the call. Jaden confirmed the underwear the victim wore appeared to be one of the sets stolen from her condo. Beyond that, they weren't much help to the CSU techs or Lang. She returned with the coroner in tow ten minutes later.

The coroner went to work, with the help of the CSU techs, who buzzed around ignoring them.

"Did you get us a uniform?" Cameron asked Lang.

Lang nodded. "McKenzie out of the Third. You're lucky. He's on the first day of his rotation. They're pulling him and giving him to you, special duty, as long as he's needed. He's good to go anytime you're ready. Or I can have him shipped over to HQ."

"Thanks. We'll pick him up at the Third. If you don't need anything more, we'll head out and meet you at HQ." Cameron could tell the blood and threats were getting to Jaden—she was much quieter than her usual self.

Lang contemplated Jaden, her stern eyes softening. "Stay safe."

He grasped Jaden's arm, pulling her out of the bedroom. They changed out of the protective gear and went outside. A slight bend in the street protected them from a direct view of the media. Cameron took the keys from Jaden, and she climbed into the backseat.

She stayed quiet until he stopped at a red light on his way to the Third Precinct.

"*Do you really think I need a babysitter?*" She sounded mentally exhausted.

"*It's not a babysitter, Jay. It's a bodyguard. Just pretend you're a famous actress who needs protection from the paparazzi.*"

That earned a soft mental laugh from her. "*Okay. How do you know this McKenzie anyway?*"

"*He watched you when you were passed out in the back of the SUV during the Meincke case.*"

"*The kid from the court house?*"

Cameron had told her he had a young patrol officer watched her while he was inside. "*Yeah. He seemed like a good kid. If you hate him, we can probably switch him out.*"

The light turned green.

"*I'm sure he'll be fine.*"

They made it to the Third Precinct, and Cam parked in the rear. He used the buzzer system, and someone inside let them in through the entrance officers used.

"Can I help you?" the booking officer asked, once they were

inside.

"We're looking for McKenzie. We were told he's waiting for us," Cameron replied. Jaden stood just behind him, something she often did to avoid having to answer questions posed to them.

"Hang on, I'll go grab him." The officer disappeared through the locked door and returned with McKenzie, who still wore his uniform.

The kid seemed a bit worried, but broke into a smile when he recognized Cameron.

"McKenzie," Cam said, offering his hand. McKenzie shook it. "Detective Olsen and Black," He nodded to Jaden. "Change into plain clothes and get your stuff. We'll wait in the SUV for you. Your car here?"

McKenzie shook his head. "Buddy drove me today."

"Good, we'll see you out there. Five minutes." Cameron led Jaden out of the station to the SUV, where she climbed into the back again.

McKenzie came out carrying a backpack and dressed in jeans, a dress shirt, and a suit jacket, his service weapon on his hip. Cameron hit the unlock button, and the kid threw the bag in the trunk. Jaden opened the door and shuffled over, indicating he should sit with her.

He climbed in and shut the door. His slight case of nerves was evident as he glanced from Cameron to Jaden. She regarded him with care.

"*What's your name?*" she asked.

The kid didn't seem to notice Jaden had used mind-speak. "Nate."

"*I'm Jaden. This is Cameron. Don't worry. We don't bite.*"

"Good to know." He flashed his smile. "Want to tell me what's going on? All I was told was to park my cruiser, that I'd been pulled for a special detail, and to wait to be picked up."

"You're on a protection detail for Detective Black. You heard about the Look-Alike Killer?"

"Yeah, I got the briefing this morning."

"Six women dead, who all looked like Jaden. They found the

sixth one this morning along with the words 'You're next, Black'. You're assigned to protect her for as long as the brass deems it necessary."

"Whatever it takes," Nate said.

Jaden smiled at him. The young officer seemed to be enraptured with her already.

"Excellent, we're on our way to HQ."

Cameron started the SUV and drove out. He blocked Jaden out so he could focus on driving. He could hear Nate's one-sided conversation, as she filled him in on the details and what he was expected to do.

He pulled into the underground garage of HQ and parked. The men climbed out. Nate did a quick survey, then opened Jaden's door, allowing her to step out. He followed him to the elevators, guiding Jaden with his hand on the small of her back. Cameron was glad he took this seriously, but at the same time, he felt a tiny stab of jealousy.

"Relax, he doesn't like me like that," Jaden said.

Cameron, distracted, replied aloud, "Like what?"

Nate scrutinized the pair, his eyes narrowing. Jaden clicked her teeth at him.

"Don't worry about it, Nate. Cameron is just being an alpha male."

She rolled her eyes and marched inside the elevator when the doors slid open. Cameron had to stop himself from sighing as he followed her. Jaden was just being snippy as a result of the stress she was under. At the same time, he was annoyed at himself for letting his personal feelings get in the way of his job.

They went to the main lobby where Cam got McKenzie a temporary pass and headed to their floor.

Lang sat at her desk, typing furiously on her computer. She held up a file as they passed her. No conversation needed. Cameron took it and kept going to the little Special Investigations office.

Ruth regarded them from the desk as he entered, followed by Jaden and Nate. She raised an eyebrow. "And who's this handsome man who followed you home?"

McKenzie went pink around the ears.

"Ruth, meet Nate McKenzie, uniform out of the Third. He'll be Jaden's bodyguard until this blows over."

"Nice to meet you, honey." She winked at Nate then turned to Cameron. "That the file from Lang?"

He nodded.

"Excellent. Some interesting trace from the first two crime scenes."

Jaden wandered to her chair and pulled out her laptop. McKenzie glanced around, seeming unsure of what to do.

"Here, handsome." Ruth reached into her drawer and pulled out a paperback novel. "Keep yourself busy. There should be another chair in the corner." Ruth tossed the book at him, and he caught it.

"Yes, ma'am." He followed Jaden to her little alcove.

Cam plunked himself into his desk chair and opened the files. He quickly reviewed. No additional DNA found at the first scene. A trace amount of silicone had been found in the victim, indicating she was raped with an object. "Interesting about the rape. Think the perp is impotent?"

"Keep reading," Ruth prompted.

He did. On the second scene, the same trace of silicon but, in addition, a single pubic hair that didn't match any others at the scene had been found lodged in the victim's throat. The silicone appeared consistent with a number of mass-market sex toys. They were still running the hair through DNA. Since it with such a small sample, they processed it traditionally, rushing it to the head of the line so the results would be back tomorrow.

"They got a hair."

"Yeah, maybe the perp isn't as savvy as we thought."

"Maybe it's another plant. This guy seems to be one step ahead of us. We've been chasing our tails for the last three days." He let out a frustrated sigh. "Did you see what the last message was?"

"'You're next, Black.'" Ruth shook her head. "Do you think

Jaden's in danger?"

"I believe she may be. I don't even have a description on this guy. How can I protect her from someone when I don't know what he looks like?"

"I can't answer that," Ruth replied. The phone rang, and she answered it.

Cameron focused on the report again. He reread it to see if he'd missed anything. He hadn't.

A knock sounded on the door, and Lang stuck her head in. "Hey, I called in some extra hands. This is Detectives Chris Muller and Logan Weber. They're tech experts." She opened the door the rest of the way. "They want to go over your computers."

Cameron smiled. "Thanks. I've worked with them before," he said as they walked into the office. Lang disappeared into the main bullpen.

Logan shook Cameron's hand. "Wow. I think this used to be a broom closet."

He laughed. "That's how I usually describe the space." He shook Chris's hand as well. "So, you're helping out the investigation, eh?"

"Yeah, we got called in." Chris winked.

"I'm glad to have the extra help." Cameron tried not to appear too smug that Lang took the bait. It helped having a couple of extra friendly faces on the case.

"*What are you two scheming?*" Jaden asked from her chair. Chris jumped at hearing from Jaden—he still wasn't used to her mind-speak.

"*Nothing, Jay.*"

"I want to take a look at your laptop," Logan replied. "We're looking for who is leaking information to the media, checking everyone's computer as a precaution."

"*Liar. Here.*" Jaden stood, and McKenzie jumped to follow her. "*Be careful with it.*" She handed it over to Logan. "*It's my baby.*"

"Thanks, I will be. Who is this?" Logan pointed to McKenzie then exchanged a glance with Chris who also raised his eyebrows.

"This is Nate McKenzie. He's a uniform out of the Third assigned to me for the moment."

Chris held out his hand, and Nate shook it, while he gave a quick once-over to Jaden, settling on her very low cut top.

"Nice to meet you, Chris Muller."

Logan stuck out the hand not holding Jaden's laptop. "Logan Weber."

Jaden glanced between all three of them, her eyes narrowing at Chris.

"Men!" she said, in a huff, she snatched the file from Cameron's desk on the way before stalking to her chair and dropping into it, hiding behind the file Nate smiled and returned to the desk chair he had been sitting in.

Logan and Chris stared at Cameron. "What was that about?" Chris asked.

"Jaden's a telepath. You guys need to learn to block," Cameron replied, shaking his head. "She could tell what you were thinking." He paused and grinned. "I could tell what you were thinking, and I'm not a telepath."

Chris blushed, and Logan laughed. They took Jaden's laptop into one of the conference rooms the rapidly growing task force had claimed it during the investigation.

Ruth ran out and got everyone lunch from the cafe around the corner. They spent the rest of the afternoon working on leads from Jaden's perspective, checking everyone she'd come in contact with recently, and working backward through her life. She went through all of the bad guys they had put away. Everyone from the new maintenance man in her building to the guy who ran her favorite delivery place.

They came up with nothing.

Chapter Seventeen

"*Why* can't I drive?" Jaden asked for the third time since they had left HQ and headed into rush hour traffic.

"For the tenth time...big evil bad guy who wants to kill you," Cameron replied, frustrated with her. She knew the reason, but that didn't stop her from pouting about it. "Get out of my head when I'm driving."

She made a frustrated noise, but waited until he stopped the SUV before she asked, "*What are we doing with him?*" She nodded toward Nate.

"He sticks with us until at least seven-thirty when we get a couple of night shift uniforms."

She clicked her teeth and settled into the seat. At the next light, she started at him again.

"*What about my laptop? I want it back.*"

"Jaden!" Cameron raised his voice. He wasn't much for shouting, but she was driving him crazy. "I know you're frustrated, but taking it out on me is not going to help the situation."

Jaden let out a exasperated sigh and crossed her arms, staring out the window. "*I'm sorry, Cam.*" Her voice was softer than normal, and he could tell Nate wasn't privy to this conversation.

"I'm sorry I yelled. I know you're hurting."

"Still, I shouldn't take it out on you. Forgive me?"

"Always, darling." He glanced at her in the rearview mirror and smiled. She returned his grin.

They pulled into the parking lot of Cameron's condo building. He parked Jaden's SUV in visitor's parking. Then he went inside, followed by Nate and Jaden.

"We're home," Cameron called as he opened the door, his nose assaulted by smells of something delicious cooking. They all entered, and he set the alarm behind them. "Paul?" he called again.

"He's not here." Jaden told him, sounding a bit worried.

"Who's not here?" Nate asked.

"Paul," Cameron replied.

Nate raised his eyebrow. "Paul...."

"It's complicated. Can I use your computer?" Jaden asked Cameron.

He nodded, and she disappeared into the office, followed by Nate. Cameron went into the kitchen and found the slow cooker stuffed with something that smelled like curry. He spotted a note on the table from Paul.

Nate came out of the office, shaking his head.

"Jay giving you a hard time?" Cameron asked him.

"It's not bad. She just bit my head off for stalking her." He flashed his killer smile. "She doesn't mean it."

"She's stressed over this whole thing, and she hates that she doesn't have her laptop. That thing goes everywhere with her. Jaden doesn't talk on the phone, so her laptop is how she communicates with people."

"Why not get a smart phone? Or a tablet?" The younger officer took a seat at the table while Cameron got himself a glass of water. He offered the jug, and Nate nodded.

"Because then someone might try and call her, and she wants a full keyboard. I've given up trying to understand her logic—just go with it. Trust me; it makes sense if you don't think too hard about it."

Nate laughed and thanked him for the water. The security alarm went off, and both men jumped, drawing their weapons. Nate beat him into the hall by a heartbeat.

"Show me your hands," he commanded, leveling his gun at Paul's chest.

Paul, for his part, jumped ten feet in the air, dropping the bag of groceries he held.

"Relax. That's Paul." Cameron pushed Nate's hands down, so the gun pointed at the floor.

The other officer holstered his weapon. "Sorry," he said, over the screeching of the alarm.

Cameron went over and disarmed it. "My fault, I didn't turn it off when I realized Paul was out."

"It's okay," Paul replied. "I don't think there was anything breakable in the bag." He regarded the squished bag of groceries then his eyes snapped to Nate. "Who are you?"

"Paul, meet Nate McKenzie. He's Jaden's new bodyguard until this blows over."

Paul shook his hand. "Nice to meet you. Usually, I prefer to know men before I allow them to point deadly objects at me."

Nate laughed.

"Are you staying for dinner?"

"I'm on duty until seven-thirty."

"Oh! Good thing I made extras."

Paul picked up the groceries and hurried into the kitchen, calling to Jaden that he was home. Nate went to check on her.

Cameron rejoined Paul in the kitchen, after the security company called his cell phone and he confirmed it was once again a false alarm. Paul dropped the groceries on the counter, then stopped and grabbed Cameron's shirt, pulling him close. The older man kissed him, his tongue exploring his mouth, before he pulled away.

"How was your day?"

"Good. I met up with some mates. Went round to the shops. Made dinner. What about your day?" He unpacked the groceries as they talked. "Anything new?"

Nate returned from the office.

"No, not really." Cameron knew Jaden had probably shared far too many details of the investigation with Paul, but he wasn't going to say anything in front of Nate.

Paul frowned. "Damn." He pulled the cover off of the slow cooker and a heavy aroma filled the room. "Do you both like Indian food?"

"Love it," Cameron replied.

"Ditto." Nate studied the condo, seeming at a loss of what to do.

"Why don't you put the TV on?" Cameron suggested to him. "I think we'll be opting for a quiet night at home."

Nate settled on some documentary that just played in the background. Jaden stayed in the office until Paul called her for supper.

Everyone settled around the table, and Paul buzzed to and fro, clearly pleased at entertaining. He opened a bottle of red wine and poured himself a generous glass. "Nate, do you want some?"

"I'm working," Nate replied. "Sorry."

"Cameron?" Paul offered.

"Sure." He knew he should refuse as he should be watching over Jaden, but Nate's sharp senses had her under a watchful eye, and he needed to relax just a tiny bit.

Paul filled his glass and sat down. Jaden held up hers.

"Did you want some water?" Paul asked her.

She threw a bun at him. "*Wine.*"

"*Oi!* Watch it," Paul replied. "Since when do you drink, luv?"

They exchanged a standoffish glare Cameron recognized it as them having a mental conversation. Paul poured her a glass of wine, and the dinner conversation focused on Paul's work in Australia running a wildlife rescue—nothing of the unpleasantness of the day.

Jaden drank enough wine to make her incredibly giggly, and they sat around the table long after dinner had finished while Cameron and Paul took turns telling stories. At last, Paul shooed everyone out, so he could clean the kitchen. They'd settled on the couch when Cameron's cell phone rang.

"Olsen," he answered.

"It's Logan. I found something," he said without preamble.

"What?"

Everyone stilled, staring at him. Cameron waved a hand and made his way into the bedroom, shutting the door to get some privacy.

"Whoever installed this phishing program is a relative genius," Logan explained. "I've been chasing down the IP routing since I got my hands on it. Looks like it was installed two years ago. Just after the computer was activated. According to the records I have, Jaden took the laptop with her to Australia during that time. I think the program was installed there."

"You think this guy has been stalking her for over two years?" Cameron was a bit flabbergasted the stalker had been active for so long. The person had been obsessed with Jaden before she even became a police officer.

"Yes. He had the information routed all over the world, Australia, South Africa, China, Russia, the UK, Canada, UK, Brazil. This guy is a world traveler," Logan explained. "I've narrowed him down to Toronto currently, but I can't get a fix. He's bounced his signal off of every free WiFi connection in the city."

"Christ, do we have any hints where he is?"

"Nothing. I've sent out a request for security footage from any of the places that have cameras, but that won't be in until the morning. I'd like to interview Jaden, though. Maybe I can get a better sense of where to look if I talk to her. If this guy has been following her for two years, she's got to have noticed something."

Jaden's loud laugh sounded from the living room.

"When were you thinking of interviewing her?"

"Tonight."

"That's not such a good idea," Cameron said. "Tomorrow."

"Why not?"

"She's had a bit too much wine with dinner."

"Is she even legal to drink?" Logan sounded surprised Jaden had been drinking.

Cameron bit back a sarcastic remark. "She's twenty, so, yes, she's legal. She's just blowing off steam. You can have her tomorrow."

"Alright." Logan sighed. "Hang on, Chris wants to talk to you."

"Hey, Cameron," the other detective said, when he came on the line. "I wanted to give you an update on the Meincke case if you're interested."

"Sure, where are you guys at?" He wanted to make sure Meincke rotted in hell, or at least in a tiny concrete cell for the rest of his life.

"He's being held without bail until the trial. They're still gathering evidence, but CSU teams have recovered eight bodies from the property," Chris explained. "They're still searching, a few are at least ten years old, based on decomposition and a few other things."

"Fuck me in the ass," Cameron muttered.

Chris laughed ironically. "Careful, someone might take you up on the offer. Anyway, this case keeps snowballing. The media hasn't gotten its teeth into it yet. They're too busy worrying about the Look-Alike Killer to pay attention to some CSU techs out in the country, digging through dirt."

"How long do you think that will last?"

Chris made a noise in the back of this throat. "Not long enough. I've got to run. We'll drop you a text tomorrow, so we can get together."

"Sure, thanks for the update, Chris." Cameron hung up the phone. He waited for a few moments, listening to the commotion in the living room, Jaden's loud giggles, and Paul's soft accent. He smiled, even with Jaden being under threat from a crazed suspect who wanted to murder her. For the first time in his life, he felt happy with his relationships.

He returned to the living room to find his two lovers had broken out the Twister game from the hall closet. Jaden lay on the floor, twisted with Paul, while Nate spun the wheel.

"Cameron," Paul exclaimed. "Grab a circle."

"I'll watch, thanks."

He settled on the couch and watched as they crawled around on the mat for the next twenty minutes, until Jaden managed to knock Paul down. She jumped in triumph, only to have Paul shove her into the overstuffed chair and a half in the corner of the living room.

She shrieked and giggled. Nate rolled his eyes.

An urgent hammering sounded on the door.

Nate and Cameron both stared at the door. McKenzie stood and drew his weapon. Keeping it pointed at the floor, he cautiously approached the door. Cameron followed, leaving his weapon holstered. The glass and a half of wine had him buzzing, and he didn't want to risk pulling his gun unless absolutely necessary.

Nate glanced through the peephole. His shoulders relaxed as he holstered his weapon and opened the door. "You scared the crap out of me, Sean." He stepped away to allow the uniform into the apartment.

"Sorry," Sean replied. "I heard a woman shriek. Scared the crap out of *me*."

The younger officer glanced at Cameron. "Detective Olsen, this is Sean O'Neil, he's a sergeant out of the Third."

"Nice to meet you." Cameron held out his hand, and O'Neil shook it. "Are you our uniform for the night?"

O'Neil shook his head. "I have two rotating cars, so there will always be someone out front. I was just coming to collect Nate."

Cameron glanced at his watch. *Almost eight. Where did the time go?* "How did you get in the building?"

"Some sweet old lady let me in," O'Neil replied with a grin. "I gave her a lecture about opening the door to strangers—even if they are in uniform."

"That's probably Kathleen. She's my upstairs neighbor. I'll have a talk with her."

O'Neil nodded. "Okay, Browne is out front, he's rotating out with Davis and her rookie, Wheeler. What time do you want McKenzie here in the morning?"

"I want to head into the office around eight—so seven-thirty," Cameron told McKenzie's superior officer, doing the mental calculations in his head.

"Sounds good. Let me grab my stuff." Nate disappeared into the apartment and returned few moments later with his jacket and bag.

"Thanks for everything, Nate. We'll see you tomorrow." He shook hands with the officer and let him and O'Neil out of the apartment, locking the door and the deadbolt after them then re-arming the security system.

He went into the living room. Paul sat on one end of the couch, Jaden's head resting on his lap with a pillow between them. She stared up at him.

"*Want to come and watch a cheesy cop show?*"

"*Sure, Jay.*"

Cameron went to sit on the oversized chair, but she lifted her feet, indicating he should sit there. He did and with a lap full of Jaden's feet. A few minutes into the program, he started absently rubbing her feet. She made mewing noises as he hit the right spot on one foot, so he kept massaging, the soft sounds she made headed straight to his groin.

Paul caught his eye, and they shared a smoldering exchange. Cameron wanted both of his lovers. Paul reached across the couch to him, his fingers brushing over his neck and collar, making goose bumps rise. Other parts of his anatomy also responded to his touch.

He shifted and adjusted slightly, continuing to rub her feet. Paul played with Jaden's hair as well, and Jaden shifted and squirmed. She excused herself to go to the bathroom during a commercial break, and while she was in there, Paul slid across the couch.

Leaning in, Cam captured his lips, kissing him. "God, I want you," he said pulling away.

"I want you, too."

Cameron glanced toward the bathroom.

"I want Jaden as well." He could feel his cheeks coloring at the admission.

"I know." Paul played with Cam's hair. "Jay and I talked about this. I'm not sure how it's going to work, because honestly I'm not into girls. I'm certainly not into her, but we're willing to go with the flow and try out a threesome kind of thing, though."

"I don't know," he whispered, unsure of taking this step.

"*Cam.*" Jaden's arms slipped over his shoulder. She leaned in close, her head pressed against his, whispering only to him. "*I've loved Paul for as long as I can remember. I know I'm never going to be with him. Paul and I have worked it out. Just let it happen.*"

He nodded at her words, and then he cleared his throat. "So we're playing Cameron in the middle?"

"*Pretty much,*" she replied, from behind the couch. He turned to face her, and she claimed him as her own with an aggressive kiss. "*You ready for this?*"

"*God, yes.*"

Cameron kissed her again. The second she pulled away, Paul found his lips, kissing him. When they broke apart, Cameron gasped for breath, struggling to comprehend what was happening.

Jaden and Paul exchanged a glance, and the older man stood, pulling Cameron to his feet. Jaden went into the bedroom first, and they followed.

He trembled as they shut the door behind them. Jaden had already stripped down to a bra and jeans when they entered the bedroom. She watched them from the middle of the room as Paul pressed him against the door, kissing him hard. His lover's hands slid lower, undoing his dress pants. He sighed in relief as his cock came free from the restrictive fabric.

His older lover's kisses were wet and sloppy. Cameron returned the favor, his hands sliding down Paul's stomach and undoing his pants. He dipped his fingers inside to stroke him. He smiled as the smaller man's mouth opened in a perfect O of pleasure. A soft moan sounded in his throat that shot right to his cock, making him harder.

He stared at his partner who stood in just a pair of the sexy underwear she favored. His gaze darted from one to the other, unsure of whom he wanted first. Paul gave him a small shove forward. He crossed the room to where Jaden stood, losing his shirt and pants along the way, just leaving him in his boxer briefs.

He kissed her again, his hands cupping her perfect breasts. His thumbs roughly massaged her nipples. She whimpered, throwing her head back, exposing her soft white neck. He kissed her there, making her jump as his lips connected with the sensitive skin.

She melted against him, allowing Cameron to lift her petite body and lay her on the bed. Kissing his way down her body, he paid special attention to her erect nipples and the side of her stomach, which made her giggle.

Her breath caught in her throat when he moved lower, his tongue teasing just under the edge of her underwear. Hands gripping at his hair, she gasped, pushing him lower. He nipped at her sensitive mound through the lacey underwear.

"Please, Cam."

He smiled at her, his fingers gripping the fabric, pulling it away. The bed dipped, and strong warm hands at his waist eased his boxer briefs off. Cam buried himself in Jaden, inhaling her sweet scent.

His mouth moved, and she moaned, her grip on his hair tightening. At the same time, his other lover spread his buttocks open.

Cameron moaned into Jaden as the older man's talented tongue probed the outer edges of his entrance. He shook with pleasure and anticipation.

He focused on his female lover, rapidly tonguing her, relishing the sting as she gripped his hair tighter and tighter, demanding more from him. He loved that she threw herself into him, no holds barred. She had to be one of the most passionate lovers he had ever had.

She groaned again. Whining as he sucked on her clit—hard.

Paul sucked on his sac, and his vision went a bit hazy. He widened his stance, and his lover honed in on his entrance.

Cameron stopped and glanced at Paul, who stopped and smiled, giving him a wink. He continued rimming him, pushing inside a bit. He moaned, his head falling forward, resting on Jaden's thigh.

He felt a soft tug on his short hair.

"*Hey,*" she demanded. "*What about me?*"

Cameron kissed her inner thigh, sucking on the spot lightly. "*Sorry, darling.*"

He worked her over again, enjoying the burst of wetness as his tongue flicked over her clit.

Paul switched from rimming him to stroking his entrance with a finger. His breath hitched as his lover added a slick cool liquid to him.

He tensed at the insistent pressure, gently opening him.

"Easy." Paul's slippery digit slid inside of him. "Just relax." He pressed a gentle kiss on the right side of Cameron's ass.

Cameron tried to focus on breathing. One hand gripped Jaden's hip, she seemed to recognize his difficulties and switched from demanding to smoothing his hair. His more experienced lover rubbed his finger against Cameron's sweet spot, drawing out his whimper.

Jaden shifted underneath him, so he rested more on her stomach than her thigh. His lover added a second finger. *Fuck*— he already felt so full. How the heck did Paul expect him to take his well-endowed cock?

"*Just relax.*" He heard Jaden in the far off reaches of his mind, her voice and presence soothing him.

The burn increased as Paul added a third finger. He made small high-pitched noises as his lover worked his ass over.

He clung to his partner, so grateful she just stayed there with him, not expecting him to do anything and not interfering either.

"Are you ready?" Paul asked.

Cameron nodded into Jaden, steeling himself against the

intrusion.

"You need to relax, Cam." Paul pulled his fingers out, and he sighed at the loss. "If you're not ready, we can wait."

He hesitated. *Did he want this?* He glanced at Jaden, her dark hair accenting her pouty lips, her brilliant green eyes burning with passion. He glanced at Paul. His blond hair stuck out in every direction. His green eyes were mirrors of Jaden's. Desire burning deep within, his chest heaved and his pre-ejaculate rolled down the edge of his thick cock. He wanted this, wanted both of them so much it hurt.

"I'm ready. I need you."

His lover moved forward until their lips met in a kiss, reaffirming their connection.

He dragged away and turned to his partner. She tugged him on top of her. *"I need you, too,"* he whispered before kissing her.

She pulled back, running her fingers though his short hair. *"How do you want to do this?"*

"I'm not sure," he replied.

"I want you in me. I want to watch while Paul fucks you." She had a wicked smile on her lips. *"I've always wanted to watch that."*

He blushed. *"Darling, I'll probably go soft."*

Jaden shushed his concerns. *"All the more reason for you to start inside me."*

She took the condom Paul handed her, ripped the packet open then stared at it in confusion.

"Here." He took it from her and showed her how it rolled on. She added a couple of extra tugs onto his prick for good measure before she settled against the pillows, smirking.

Cameron shifted to his knees, sliding a finger inside of her wet and warm heat. He couldn't wait to be buried inside of her. Paul leaned in close, his cock brushing against Cameron's ass. He turned his head and captured his lover's lips before he pulled away. Paul gave a couple of pulls on his own cock, and sat toward the end of the bed, content to wait until Cameron gave him the okay.

Jaden pulled him to her and his fingers slipped out. He wiped them on the covers before settling between her legs. He kissed her, exploring her mouth as she guided him into her. He slid in deep, and her breath hitched. Settling in, he continued to kiss her while he moved, creating a delicious friction between them. Small moans sounded in her throat every time he pressed in deep. His movement slowed then stopped when Paul kneeled behind him.

A soft kiss pressed into the middle of his back. He waited as a gentle finger slipped inside him then out again.

"Ready?" his lover asked, accent thicker than usual.

Cameron could tell he was barely hanging on to his control. "Yeah."

He leaned into Jaden, the blunt tip of his lover's cock pressing into him. Burying his face into his partner's neck, he moaned into her, the pressure already intense.

"It's okay," Paul soothed. "Relax." He pulled out then into him again, adding more lube. "You're doing great."

Cameron relaxed, grateful he had buried his cock deep inside Jaden. Her muscles contracted around him, her hands in his hair keeping him grounded and so very aroused.

"*Breathe*," she reminded him. "*You're so sexy like this.*"

He made a noise in his throat, a high-pitched whine as Paul slid inside him then stopped moving, waiting for what seemed like ages. He eased out, then thrust in again, and waited some more. The pressure drove him crazy. It brought him to the brink of pain and pleasure. It felt so good and hurt just enough, all at the same time. He felt like his body had been pushed into overload.

His heart pounded in his ears as Paul slid all the way inside him. He felt wild, pressed between his two lovers. His lover, hard and thick, buried deep inside of him; his partner, hot, wet and so very soft. Paul rubbed circles on his back while Jaden ran her fingers through his hair and kept whispering about how sexy he looked, how she loved the sounds he made. He surprised himself that even with the intense pressure, he stayed rock hard. Jaden shifted beneath him, squirming, moving her hips, begging him to resume fucking her.

Cameron lifted himself off her a little bit, allowing her to breathe again. When he moved again, they kissed. He let out a hiss as Paul moved with him. He pulled out of Jaden, almost all the way, and Paul stayed buried deep inside him. When he thrust into Jaden, Paul slid out. Together, they found a soft rhythm.

They moved in an intricate dance, but far too soon Cameron felt his orgasm rising. Jaden's tight muscles and Paul's thick cock pressing against his prostate driving him closer and closer to the edge.

He tried to verbalize his impending release, but he didn't need to. Jaden had already read his mind and increased the movement in her hips.

"*I need you. I am so close,*" she begged.

Cameron tried to focus on her. He increased his thrusts, his own climax starting to wash over him.

"That's it," his lover grunted as Cameron trapped his cock in a hot vice. "Come for me."

Cameron let go, losing control. He moved hard into his partner, and she gasped, arching, rhythmically contracting around him. Cameron's orgasm hit him hard. He called out, not caring whether he made sense or not. His body shook as his hot sticky liquid filled the condom he wore. He collapsed onto Jaden, barely able to balance on his elbows so he didn't crush her. Paul shuddered behind him, his hands tight on his hips relaxing. He waited before pulling out and collapsing to one side.

Cameron kissed his partner and moved off her. He landed on the bed, face first, tingles of pleasure still shooting though his body. He couldn't form any real thoughts other than how utterly satisfied he felt at that exact moment.

Paul slid out of bed, returning with a warm cloth to clean him. He just managed to pull off the used condom and throw it into the wastebasket before collapsing onto the bed. Jaden had moved at some point and returned wearing one of his workout shirts. He rolled onto one side and cuddled her close to him.

"*I love you,*" he thought only to her.

Jaden turned enough so they could kiss.

"*I love you, too,*" she whispered once they broke apart. She snuggled into his embrace and fell asleep.

Paul rejoined them in bed. He kissed the nape of Cameron's neck. "Can I tell you something?" he murmured in his ear.

"Sure."

"I think I love you." His forehead pressed into Cameron's shoulder. "I know it's only been a few days and there is so much more going on, but I think I love you."

He took in the information. It wasn't a shock to him—he'd known this was coming, mostly because he felt the same way. "I think I love you, too."

Paul kissed his neck one last time and relaxed against him. Together, they all slept, and for the first time in a very long time, none of them dreamt.

④

Cameron stood in the shower, water pounding on his back, cascading lower as he tried to wash away some of the soreness from the previous night's escapades.

The buzzer to his apartment rang.

"*Who is it?*" he asked his partner, not wanting to yell over the noise of the shower and the fan.

"*It's Nate,*" she responded, sounding exhausted. "*Paul's getting it.*"

"I'll be out in a minute."

He could feel her mental shrug as she replied, "*Take your time.*"

He did, walking out of his bedroom at five to eight. Paul stood in the kitchen, flipping pancakes, his hair still damp from his earlier shower.

"How many do you want?" The older man pulled another overflowing plate from the oven. "I have lots."

"Just two is fine."

At the counter, Cameron sat next to Jaden who picked at a

pancake on her plate. Nate looked as if he had tucked away several and worked on finishing the last one.

Paul gave Cam three large ones. "You know, if you stick around much longer, I'm going to get fat," he teased the older man, who poured maple syrup on the plate.

"Naw, just trying to make up for all of the calories you burned last night." His lover winked.

Cameron could feel himself blush, not that McKenzie noticed as he filled his plate with more pancakes.

"*You would think no one ever fed him before.*" Jaden wrinkled her nose, teasing the young officer.

Nate responded with a nod. "I'm a beat cop. Never turn down free food, and eat when you can 'cause it might be the last chance you have for the shift."

Jaden patted the younger officer's blond hair. "*Don't worry. I promise we'll have lunch.*"

"Really?" Nate brightened and devoured the plate in front of him.

"*So, tell us a bit more about yourself.*" Jaden picked at the food, trying to divert attention away from herself.

McKenzie shrugged, "Not much to tell. Born and raised just outside of Toronto, did a four-year undergrad at U of T before joining the academy."

"What's your degree in?" Paul stood on the other side of the counter, munching away on the food he just finished making.

Nate cleared his throat and mumbled something.

"Sorry didn't catch that," the older man teased.

"Music."

Jaden giggled. "*What did you study?*"

The young man shot her a glare.

"*Harp?*" Jaden giggled again and almost fell off her stool.

Nate shook his head at her. Cameron couldn't hear their conversation but knew one was taking place.

At last, Paul interrupted the pair. "So, Nate, anyone special in your life?"

McKenzie shook his head. "My last serious girlfriend dumped

me when I joined the academy, wasn't cut out to be a cop's wife." He grabbed the last pancake. "Haven't had a girl stick around for more than a few months since then."

Cameron nodded, agreeing with Nate's sentiment.

Jaden reached over and hugged the young man. "*You're a great guy. The perfect girl is out there for you.*"

Nate patted her on the head. "Thanks, Jay."

She smiled, and resumed picking at her food. She stared at the time and sighed. "*We should start out for HQ soon.*"

"Agreed." He finished the last of his pancakes, and Paul took the plates away.

The other two left the apartment, and he paused, kissing Paul senseless before following them down to the SUV. He drove while Jaden sat in the back with Nate, much to her general annoyance.

When they arrived on their floor, a flurry of activity surrounded them. Three murders in a row, and the break had everyone speculating, especially the media, that Jaden would be the next target. He hoped Logan and Chris would be able to come up with something from Jaden's computer, because standard forensics had given them nada at the moment.

He fell into the mess and the chaos, grateful for the interruption when his phone vibrated at ten till nine with a text message. *Meet us at the coffee shop around the corner. Bring Jay.*

"*Who wants us to meet them?*" Jaden had been monitoring his thoughts when he read the message.

"Logan and Chris. I think they have some questions for you," Cameron replied. McKenzie didn't seem to be paying attention to them, so he added, "*Logan found something on your laptop last night. He wants us to meet him at the coffee shop around the corner...discreetly.*"

"*Of course.*" Jaden poked Nate in the shoulder, and, leaning over to him, they had a conversation Cam couldn't hear.

"Ruth, Jay's going a bit stir-crazy. We're going to go out on a coffee run. Is there anything we can get you?"

Ruth gave him a stern examination as though she didn't quite believe him. "No thanks, hon. Just don't stay out too long. You'll drive Lang to drink if she comes looking for you and you're not here."

"We'll be fine. We're going to the coffee shop, and we have Nate. What could possibly go wrong?"

Chapter Eighteen

*W*hen they got to the coffee shop, Logan and Chris had already claimed the back corner with the comfortable couch and chairs. Jaden and McKenzie sat with Logan, while Cameron and Chris went to get their drinks.

"You know, I've been wondering something," Cameron said as they joined the line—it seemed a bit long for being mid-morning on a weekday.

"What?" Chris shuffled forward a foot.

"Who's Noel? I remember you mentioned him as a cover, but is he really your child or...?" Cameron asked.

The other detective grinned. "He's real. It's a bit complicated. I started seeing Noel's Mom when he was three, maybe four months old. We dated for a month or two. She had used before she got pregnant. She got clean the second she found out she was expecting, but after being sober for just over a year, she began using again."

"Ouch." Never easy to see someone you loved spiral downward with drugs.

"Yeah, I tried to help for a while, but I finally called CPS and had Noel removed from his mother's care. I found him a great foster home. He's still there. His mom lost parental rights when Noel was three, just before we found out he had a childhood form of leukemia. He battled hard for a year and a half. It was tough, but he's been well for about a year. I was there through everything. I've been trying to adopt Noel since he was three."

"Why the hold up, if I can ask?"

Chris shrugged. "They wouldn't let me adopt him while he was sick, and now that he's better, there has been a setback or two." He glanced toward Logan. "I'm hoping it will go through sooner rather than later. In the meantime, his foster mom is the best about keeping our relationship strong. She lets me see him as often as I can and even take him for weekends and overnight when I'm not working." Chris got that goofy expression on his face most parents got when they talked about their kids. "He's great."

"He sounds like it. Congratulations."

They made it to the front of the line, and Muller put in the order, then Cameron added in his. Chris insisted on paying. They carried the drinks to the table, and Cameron went to get sugar and milk for Jaden.

He sat down in a chair, turning it so it faced the door a bit more.

"As I was saying," Logan said, nodding toward Cameron, bringing him into the conversation, "we need a list of people who have been in your life for the past two years."

"That's going to be a long list. Just work alone has to be close to a hundred people, not to mention friends, acquaintances, relatives." She trailed off, thinking hard.

"Why don't we start with the people you have the most contact with and go backward from there?" Logan suggested. Chris had a notepad out, taking notes on everything Jaden said.

"Well, pretty much it's Cameron and Ruth then Paul."

Cameron's head spun by the time she finished listing as many people as she could. He had no idea his partner had so many contacts all over the world—from a childhood friend in Ottawa, to a distant cousin in Italy, to a friend in Japan who she met in high school, to an Internet friend she'd had for seven years who lived in Georgia.

Chris worked on patterns—who could be involved and who to exclude. Jaden excused herself to the bathroom. McKenzie stood to follow her, but she waved him off. "It's just around the corner. I'll be fine."

McKenzie glanced at him for permission, and he nodded. His partner huffed and stomped off to the restrooms.

"You know, we haven't looked at one angle," Cameron pointed out, as Logan and Chris discussed all the people Jaden mentioned.

"What's that?" Logan asked.

"Someone saw Jaden and started stalking her. It happens, especially to celebrities, but not unheard of with others. It would explain an obsession that's coming to a head after what the perp views as a long-standing courtship."

Chris went to reply but paused until a dark-haired woman had passed by their table and moved out of hearing range.

"True, but it could also be someone who's close to Jaden, and she's just not seeing their obsession, or is seeing it in a different way because she's been involved with them for so long. Take her Internet friend for example. They've known each other for seven years, and neither of them has even considered meeting each other. That screams of one or both of them lying."

"Or just being happy with their relationship and not wanting to ruin a good thing by seeing what the person is like in real life." Cameron wanted to say more, but his cell phone rang. He pulled it out, and the caller ID displayed Lang's number. "Olsen."

"Where are you?" She sounded exasperated.

"At the coffee shop, blowing off steam. Why?" he snapped, equally annoyed at Lang for acting as if they were children out after curfew.

"Get back here. Now."

"Why?" His heart skipped a beat. Had they found a seventh body?

"We got the DNA back on that hair. It was from a woman."

"Did you compare it to Jaden's?"

"Of course. Not a match. But there is a familial match to her friend Paul. I want her back here now. I'm sending a uniform to collect Paul and bring him in for questioning. There is definitely something more going on."

"Are we talking siblings?"

If it came from a sibling, how did the perp get one of Adeline's hairs? Could this be about Adeline and have nothing to do with Jaden herself?

"No," Lang said, halting that train of thought for him. "Not enough markers match, nor for a parent. We're thinking a first cousin."

Did Paul have any cousins? He had mentioned his aunt raised him but hadn't mentioned any cousins. He would have to ask Jaden when she returned from the bathroom. "Okay, I'll get Jaden and head to the office."

Lang made a huff of annoyance, and hung up. He relayed the information to Chris and Logan.

"Speaking of Jaden, she's taking a long time in the bathroom." McKenzie glanced at his watch. "It's been almost ten minutes."

"She can take ages sometimes." Just as the words left his mouth, his cell phone rang for a second time. The number popped up as his home. "Hey, Paul."

"Where's Jaden?" His lover sounded slightly panicked.

"She's in the bathroom. Why?"

"Check. Please."

He covered the mouthpiece of the cell. "Nate, go check on Jaden," he ordered and snapped to Paul. "What's wrong?"

"I don't know. I usually can feel her like a soft tingly presence in the back of my head, but all of a sudden she was gone."

McKenzie came returned, his eyes frantic, searching the coffee shop, his hand on his gun. "She's gone. Jaden is gone."

His body went numb. *Gone? How can she be gone? She just went to the bathroom.*

"I'll call you back." He hung up his cell. "How can she be gone?" he asked Nate.

Chris and Logan stood, and Cameron followed.

"There's a rear entrance I didn't realize was there." McKenzie told him, sounding terrified.

Cameron swore. He dialed Ruth.

"Jaden's gone." He resisted the urge to run into the bathroom and check. If Nate said she was gone, he believed him.

"What? Gone where?" Ruth demanded. "Did she just take off?"

"I don't know. Trace her."

"How? She doesn't carry a cell."

He swore again, loudly.

"Cameron," Logan said, "we need to call Lang and get her a team out here ASAP. You and I both know Jaden wouldn't have just taken off. Not when she's got a killer after her."

"Call everyone, Ruth. I want uniforms and detectives here in two minutes." Cameron jammed the buttons on the phone.

"Chris, go talk to the manager and see if they have cameras on the back door. Logan, don't let anyone else leave the coffee shop. They might have seen something."

The two detectives dispersed on his orders.

"Nate, cover the rear door."

It took another thirty seconds before two police cars came screaming to the front of the coffee shop. They entered then took orders from Logan. One went outside, circling around to the alley in the off chance the perp hadn't gotten away yet.

Lang arrived a minute later. She took over the scene, barking commands. They interviewed people who'd been in the vicinity and might've seen something. The shop swam before Cam, everything going a bit fuzzy. Chris returned with a USB stick.

"They have video surveillance of the perp," he said. "It was a woman who put something over her mouth and dragged her out."

"Did she struggle?" Guilt threatened to overwhelm him. He shouldn't have waved McKenzie off when she wanted to go to the bathroom. He should have taken her himself. This was all his fault.

"Briefly. It might have been something like chloroform. If it was, that's a pretty controlled substance. We'll be able to trace it,"

Chris replied.

Lang joined them, and he handed her the USB stick, explaining the situation.

"Do you know where Paul is? I have a feeling he knows a lot more than he thinks he knows," Lang said.

Shit. Paul. He'd hung up on him.

"He's at my condo." He ran his fingers through his hair. "Fuck!"

"I'll send a car to bring him to HQ I have some serious questions for him. In the meantime, McKenzie," she said, and the young officer snapped to attention. "Take Cameron back to the office. Don't let him out of your sight."

"Yes, ma'am."

Lang all but pushed him and Nate out the door while Chris and Logan stayed behind to help control the scene.

He made it to the homicide floor, and everyone avoided them, except for one detective.

"Well, well, looks like Ms. Detective of the year isn't so perfect after all," Detective Bill Wilson said with a smug smirk on his face. "Getting herself kidnapped by a killer. I'm betting this is all a big publicity stunt."

He didn't have the patience for him today. "Fuck off, Wilson."

Wilson stood, stuck his chest out, and tried to suck in the beer belly hanging well over his gun belt. "Make me."

He attempted to push past him, but when Wilson tried to stop him, Cameron leveled the older detective with a single punch.

Cameron leaned over him. "I said, fuck off."

"Fuck you," Wilson cried from the floor, holding his nose. "I think it's broken."

He shrugged and stepped over him, followed by McKenzie as he made his way to their tiny inner office. He passed Captain Grigorva, who didn't say anything despite witnessing the fight.

Ruth sat at her desk, with her phone ringing off the hook, when he stepped inside. They closed the door, shutting out the rest of the office. She stopped answering her phone and stood.

"Cam." Tears welled in her eyes.

He walked to her and hugged the older woman. "We'll get her back, I promise. We need to focus on the details. There has to be something there."

Ruth pulled away, sucking in a deep breath. "You're right. Stiff upper lip. We'll get through this."

He gave her a pretending punch in the shoulder. "That's my girl. Let's work on it."

Ruth dropped into her chair and started typing, ignoring the row of phone lines that blinked in sequence.

"So, I compiled all of the footage Logan had pulled from different places with free WiFi across the city. Now that I know we're looking for a woman, and I got a still photo from the footage Chris just sent me, I was able to do a facial-recognition search. I found several instances of this woman in different locations at different times. Most disturbingly of all"—she keyed up footage—"this is last Monday, coffee shop a couple of blocks away. Jaden has just run out of the shop, and as you are following her, this woman comes in."

Ruth pointed to the footage of a dark-haired woman entering the coffee shop just as Cameron hurried out past her.

"Holy fuck." He hadn't even noticed her at the time. "Show me the screen cap of her from earlier today again."

Ruth pulled it up, and he cursed. The woman had been at the coffee shop two days prior when he met with Logan and Chris, and she had walked past them moments before they realized Jaden was missing.

"Do we have any idea who she is?" Ruth asked, staring at the screen cap.

"According to forensics, she's Paul's cousin."

"Me cousin?" Paul said, sounding shocked, his typically muted accent in full swing. Shit, Cameron hadn't noticed him entering the office or standing there listening. "Which one?"

"How many do you have?" Cameron faced him. His lover looked like utter hell. His hair stuck up—probably from running his fingers through it one too many times—and he had a haunted appearance about him.

"First cousins, eight. Second cousins, not sure. Maybe twenty, twenty-five. Too many to count after that."

"Female, first cousins," he prompted.

"Three. Two older, one younger. Katherine and Cindy both live in London. Married with kids and grandkids even. Amy is the youngest, single, a pharmaceutical rep. She works all over the world for a company that sells HIV drugs."

Cameron stepped away from the monitor. "Is that Amy?"

Paul's jaw dropped. He stared at the screen, stunned. He nodded, then shook his head, then nodded again.

"What's Amy's last name?"

"Fitzpatrick. Amy Elizabeth Fitzpatrick," Paul said, still appearing shocked.

"Ruth, send the information to Lang. I want a BOLO. Pull any immigration records for her."

Ruth had started the search before the words were out of his mouth, her fingers flying over her computer keys.

"Amy couldn't have done this," the older man protested. "She loves Jaden. She even spent last Christmas with us."

Dammit, that's when the video cameras had been installed. He stared down his lover. "Paul, we've moved past that. You have a choice—either help us find Amy and Jaden or go home and wait. I don't have time to argue with you."

Paul swallowed a couple of times, his Adam's apple bobbing. "I'll help."

"Good, you need to talk with Lang. She'll be able to work things from that side of the investigation. I'm going to run down ways to trace Jaden," he told him. "If she's been drugged, she won't be able to help from her end."

"I'll do my best," Paul replied.

"McKenzie, you stick with Paul. Don't let him out of your sight."

"Yes, sir." Nate snapped to attention.

The pair left the office to go talk with Lang. Cameron sat down to work with Ruth, praying it wasn't too little, too late.

Chapter Nineteen

"You should go home." Lang stood over him, her arms crossed.

The clock on Cam's computer read well after seven, and so far, they had heard nothing from Jaden. Canvases had come up empty. A security camera a block away had recorded Amy driving a dark-red, paneled van away from the scene, and the plates came back stolen. There were no reports of any vans at the other crime scenes. Amy had stolen it specifically to kidnap Jaden.

She was cunning, organized, and—worst of all—she was three steps ahead of them.

"I'm not going home until we find Jaden."

"There is nothing left you can do tonight. I know it's hard, but go home. Take Paul and try to get some sleep." Lang seemed worried about them. "Being dead exhausted when we need you fresh isn't going to help Jaden."

He closed his eyes, knowing she was right, but he just didn't want to admit it. "Come on, Lang. Another hour and I can look through more video to see if we can catch the van heading in a specific direction."

"Go home, Cameron. Or I'm calling Novak."

Ruth had been listening in to the conversation from her

cubicle and stuck her head around the corner. "Rhonda is right, sweetie. Go home. Try and relax."

He ran his fingers over his face in frustration. "How can I relax when a crazed killer has Jaden?"

"You need to try, Cam," Ruth replied. "Please. For me."

"Alright. For you."

He gathered his things and grabbed Nate and Paul from the conference room. McKenzie drove them to Cameron's place. They spent the ride in silence, anxiety pressing down on them. Lang must have called ahead because a patrol car sat in front of his building when they arrived.

Nate pulled into Cameron's parking spot and made them stay in the car until he returned from speaking with the officers. "They cleared the area. We're okay to go in."

They went inside, McKenzie shutting and locking the door to the condo behind them. Paul wandered into the bedroom, ignoring both officers. Cameron went to the fridge. Unable to do anything else, he pulled a beer from the fridge and downed it in three gulps.

"You want one?" he offered to McKenzie.

"Working," Nate replied. "Are you sure you want to be drinking?"

He shot the young officer a glare. "Are you sure you don't want to be drinking?"

Paul came into the kitchen, and Cameron held up a beer for him. His lover accepted it, drinking just as quickly as Cameron had.

"We should eat something." Paul pointed out as he started on his second beer.

"Not hungry, don't feel like cooking," Cameron replied.

"Neither am I," the older man admitted.

"Pizza?" Nate suggested. "We could order in."

"Lang would have a hissy fit." He opened the third beer, his swallows deep and needy, and finished it. "She wants us under lock and key in case this has something to do with...." Cam set his jaw, not saying any more.

"To do with you and Jay sleeping together," Nate finished, and shrugged when Cam shot him a stone-faced glare. "She told me that could be a reason all of this began. Why don't we order from the cop joint over on St. Clair? If you order them a couple of mediums, I know some patrol guys who would bring it to us."

Cameron thought it over for a minute. "God, I remember doing that when I was in patrol. One car used to pick up five or six and drive around, delivering to all the other cars." He gave a short bitter laugh. "Sure, why not."

Nate sent a text to one of his buddies on patrol, who agreed to deliver the pizza if they got one for him. He ordered four, two for them, one for his buddy picking up the pizza, and one for the car out front, which would be there for the entire night.

The pizza arrived, and Nate accidentally set off the alarm when he opened the door. Hot and greasy, the pizza was the kind he would usually be all over, but Cameron ate without tasting it. He finished his sixth beer and crashed out on the couch with Paul. McKenzie left around nine with the promise to return first thing in the morning. His lover moved off the couch at ten-thirty.

"We should try and get some sleep."

"Do you think you'll be able to find Jaden in Dreamworld?" Cameron asked.

He had wanted to know all day, but with so many people around he hadn't dared ask. Paul shifted beneath him, snuggled into his chest.

"Maybe. If she's been drugged, it will be a lot harder to finder her than if she is clear-headed. I haven't been able to reach her since she went missing, so I'm thinking it's the former."

"You can reach into Dreamworld even when you're not asleep?" Surprised rattled through him at this revelation.

"That's why I'm a Dream Master. Jaden can control the Dreamworld, but only when she is asleep, and she doesn't always reach that realm. I can be in the Dreamworld and in the real world at the same time."

"So, it's like astral dreaming?" Cameron struggled to understand how this all worked. He'd always accepted Jaden's gift as something tangible. She could read his mind and use hers to speak to him, simple enough. It might be a bit mad, but at least he could put his finger on it. Paul's talent seemed much more obscure.

"No, Dreamworld and astral dreaming are two different things." Paul shifted so he stared at Cameron. "With astral dreaming, you're walking around the waking world in an out-of-body experience. Or you travel to the astral plane. In the Dreamworld, you're fully asleep. No cord connecting you. It's a place where minds meet and control. No rules and typically no real-life consequences."

"Right." He struggled to process the information.

"So, if we get some sleep, we might be able to reach Jaden." Paul sat upright, stretching. "Come on."

His lover pulled him off the couch. He turned the lights off and double-checked the locks before joining Paul in the bedroom. Cam stripped, leaving his boxer briefs, and brushed his teeth and washed his face before climbing between the covers. Paul crawled in next to him once he finished in the bathroom. Naked.

Cameron raised an eyebrow. "Aren't you a bit underdressed?"

"Huh?" Paul stared at him, his brows drawn in confusion, but then the light bulb went on. "Oh, I always sleep like this."

"Oh, I thought.... Never mind." He went to move away, but the older man stopped him.

"You thought I'd want sex while Jaden is out there somewhere missing?"

"Sorry, it was stupid."

"Not stupid. You're worried about her. I am, too."

"I'm afraid I won't see her again." Tears burned in his eyes.

"Hey." Paul moved forward, kissing him. "We'll get her back. I promise."

He didn't answer but pressed his mouth to Paul's. Twisting away, he turned off the light on the nightstand. They cuddled together, and, to his surprise, Cameron found himself drifting off to sleep.

☙

Cold seeped in from the edges of the cave. He looked up from the gold mound he lay on. Jaden and Paul were both missing.

I'm alone. Cameron huffed, and fire shot from his nostrils, smoke filling the cavern. Closing his eyes, he did his best to drift off to sleep.

☙

The thick fog obscured the path ahead of Cam He inhaled, relishing the woody, earthen scent. He didn't spend as much time as he wanted at his cabin in the Muskokas. The property sat on a gorgeous private lake with a handful of rentals, but the same families had owned most of the old cabins for as long as anyone could remember.

He loved his cottage. He kept walking, and the cabin loomed out of the fog and the darkness. The lights were on. Funny—he didn't remember leaving the lights on. He climbed the steep hill to where the cabin overlooked the water. It seemed to take ages to reach the top. Feeling winded, he stopped, sucking in some deep breaths.

It would have to be on this time of year—too cold otherwise. The building had no central heating, but a large potbellied stove in the cabin's main room along with a fireplace in the master bedroom kept the place comfortable. The rest of the rooms were equipped with heavy quilts and the occasional space heater. Not that he used the place at this time of year, usually. He still hadn't had a chance to shut it down for the winter. He'd hoped for at least one more trip before he had to pull the dock in and winterize the pipes.

As he took a few more steps toward the cabin, the smell of wood smoke seemed to get thicker. *Who started the fire in the stove?* The previous Thanksgiving had been the last time someone visited him here in the mountains. His sister had driven to the cabin with his two nieces, and they'd spent the day cooking the turkey in the wood stove. Everyone had snuggled in the master bedroom because the other rooms had been freezing that night.

He reached the lower deck. The chairs were stacked underneath the upper deck, protected from the weather when he wasn't there. It seemed funny to him. The first thing he usually did was pull the chairs out from under the deck. Did that mean he wasn't here before? If he wasn't here, then why did he smell smoke and why were the lights on? He went up the stairs to the upper deck. The main door stood shut, but he could see inside to the great room. The sun disappeared over the horizon, and the cabin seemed to glow in the darkness.

Jaden moved around the cabin, an apron wrapped around her waist, adding more wood to the stove in the kitchen. He opened the door and walked inside.

"Cameron." She sounded surprised. "What are you doing here?"

"This is my cabin."

"Oh, I'm making dinner." She stopped and stared at a bowl with flour in it. "I think I'm making dinner."

"Jaden." Cameron crossed the kitchen, placing his hands covered hers. Her skin felt cold, almost icy in fact. *Something else is wrong. This is Dreamworld.* The realization hit him like a ton of bricks. *So if this is Dreamworld, then something is very wrong.* Jaden appeared just as she did in the waking world. Young, edgy, stylish. "How did you get here?"

"I don't know." She glanced around the cabin. "Where am I?"

"We're in Dreamworld."

"I thought this was your cabin." Her brows knitted.

"It is, darling." He reached over and brushed the hair from her face. A large scrape marred her forehead, as if someone had hit her over the head with something. He led her to the couch and sat down with her. "Tell me the last thing you remember."

"The last thing I remember was...." she paused, frowning. "I was cold."

"Okay, you remember you were cold. What else? A sound? A smell? Was it light? Dark?"

Jaden shook her head. "No. Maybe? I don't know." Tears welled in her eyes. "I feel like there is something so important I have to tell you, but I don't know what it is."

"Shh," Cameron soothed. "It's okay, you'll remember." He held her close, amazed her body was still freezing cold, even with the stove pumping out heat to the great room.

She stayed silent for a while then tensed all of the sudden and pulled away from him. "Paul. Where is Paul?"

"I don't know, Jay. He wasn't with me when I got here."

Tears sprang into her eyes. "She wants him, too."

"Who wants him?"

Jaden seemed like she wanted to say something on the tip of her tongue, then she shook her head. "I don't know."

"It's okay."

She shivered. "It's so cold in here. I even threw more wood on the fire, but it's not helping."

"Your hands are like ice."

"There was ice in the water. In the water I was drinking, there was ice in it."

"Okay." He didn't want to interrupt her thoughts.

"It tasted funny though, like medicine." Jaden opened her mouth a few times, as if she tasted the drink again. "I didn't want to drink it, but she made me. Said it would stop me from dreaming."

"It didn't work, Jay. You're dreaming."

"How can I be dreaming when I'm awake?"

"You just are, darling."

"My head feels so funny, like something is wrong, like I'm missing something, something big." Her gaze darted from the kitchen to the table, then to the large picture windows overlooking the lake. Her focus slid to the hall leading to the bedrooms. "There is something down there."

Jaden rose to her feet travelled into the hall. He followed her. The temperature seemed to drop ten degrees. The hallway became almost pitch black, the light from the big room seeming to disappear. His eyes had a hard time adjusting to the dim light. By memory, he knew the two doors on the right led to the small bedrooms, the first door on the left led to the bathroom, and the second door on the left led to the master bedroom.

Jaden walked to the end of the hall. "There is something here."

She opened the door to the master bedroom. Nothing. Then to the first small bedroom. She shook her head, stalked down the hall, and opened the door to the second bedroom. Again, nothing. She turned and stared at the bathroom door, then opened it and went in. Cameron followed. She glanced around at the dated toilet and sink, the tub-shower combo with its pea-green tiles and plain beige shower curtain.

Something was there, something he was missing. Jaden went over to the door to the utility room. It opened with a loud groan.

The shape of the old water heater stood out against one wall. Against the other, the old fridge he kept for beer hummed loudly. The storage shelves were filled with oddly shaped items that created unusual shadows, but it all seemed so familiar, so normal to him.

He opened the old fridge to allow a narrow beam of light into the space. Jaden paced in the tiny room, two steps forward, two back. The floorboards creaked when she walked over a spot next to the water heater. It squeaked again.

Cameron dragged his brain. *What is so special about this room?* Thoughts ran wild through his mind, and he tried to put them into some sort of order. Why would he be led here in Dreamworld, to a place he knew but hadn't been thinking about? Why would Jaden be so attracted to the tiny corner of his cabin he only visited when he turned off the heater for the winter and drained the pipes?

He paused. The pipe cleanout in the crawlspace, and the access panel in the floor next to the hot water heater. He dropped to his knees and felt around on the floor for the latch. When he found it, he grasped it and pulled.

The narrow light illuminated part of the space. The person lying in the space moaned and moved, revealing Jaden's deathly pale face.

Chapter Twenty

*C*ameron woke with a start, his whole body shaking. The remains of the dream swirled in his head, and he scrambled awake, trying to make sense of it. Next to him, his lover moaned in his sleep.

He reached over and shook him. "Paul. Paul, wake up."

He groaned, turning over. "Huh?" he mumbled into the pillow.

"Wake up."

Paul moved, flipping the light on and blinding them both for a moment. "What's going on?"

"I know where Jaden is." He climbed out of bed, went to his dresser, and pulled out a pair of jeans and socks. Yanking them on, he grabbed a sweater from his closet. "I think she's at my cabin in the Muskokas."

"How do you know this?" Paul hadn't moved from the bed.

"I saw it in Dreamworld."

"Cameron, stop. You weren't in Dreamworld. Slow down, tell me exactly what happened."

He ran through the dream in as much detail as he could remember. The dream had already started to go fuzzy around the edges, unlike his previous Dreamworld experiences that were still crisp and new. Paul listened with rapt attention, asking the bare minimum of questions.

"So, I think the whole thing was a dream telling me where Amy had Jaden."

Paul shook his head. "I don't know. I was in Dreamworld. I left you asleep in the cave then I went out looking. I didn't see you or Jaden there. I think you just had a normal dream."

Cameron finished dressing and sat on the edge of his bed. He shook his head. "I remember clearly being in the cave, as a dragon, alone. Then I was at my cabin."

"Without Jaden or me to anchor you, you probably slipped out of Dreamworld and into REM sleep. The cave is a gateway to Dreamworld. Different people have different gateways. Our natural dream guide is a dragon, so we find ourselves in a cave. If your natural dream guide was a bear, you could find yourself in the forest. I don't think you have the ability to control Dreamworld without one of us, so what you just experienced was a regular old normal dream."

"I knew it didn't feel like Dreamworld," Cam snapped, "but I don't think it was something my brain just decided to create. If she is at the cabin, then how did she get there? I never even mentioned my cabin to Jaden. I've never taken her there. How could Amy know it existed if Jaden didn't? Also how did she get in? The road to the lake is barred and only key holders can access it. Plus my cabin is locked up tight."

"Who has keys for the cabin?"

"Just me. They're in the cupboard in the kitchen." He stood and went into the kitchen. Paul followed a moment later, walking through the apartment naked. Cam went to the cupboard where he kept the random things he would need: extra keys for his car, old cell phones, and a mug full of pens. The empty hook that usually held his keys haunted him. "The keys are gone."

"Are you sure?" Paul helped him search through the cupboard and any other place they might be hiding, but they couldn't locate them. "Could anyone have taken the keys? When was the last time you saw them?"

Cameron thought aloud. "Two weeks ago, just before we

caught the Meincke case. I spent a few days up there. I know I put the keys back in the cupboard when I got home. No one else had access to my apartment, let alone the keys. The only person who knows about the cabin besides my sister and her family is an ex-girlfriend I took there just after I bought it."

Cameron ran his fingers over his face and through his hair. He started thinking backward in a linear fashion. What had happened the night before? They'd watched TV, ate pizza Nate had a fellow police officer deliver. The stupid house alarm, which he usually didn't use, had gone off when he opened the door. It explained why he kept forgetting about it—they didn't even call to check on him to make sure it was a false alarm.

Wait—that wasn't right. They had to call if his alarm went off. He checked his cell phone. No call. Something didn't sit right.

"Did my security company call the house phone to ask if there was an emergency when my alarm went off last night?"

Paul shook his head. "No, I don't think so. Why?"

"Because they always call."

Cameron went to the front door and ensured he had it alarmed before he unlocked and opened it. The alarm screeched the moment he opened the door. It didn't take long for the patrol officer out front to buzz. Cameron let him in. They let the alarm ring for the full five minutes before it automatically switched into silent mode. He waited another two before he called his security company. They hadn't received an alarm from his residence. He had them double check, and they even tried to send a remote message to his system, only to have to the message set off another alarm in the building. Somewhere between the panel and the phone line, a bypass loop in the system had been created, stopping it from alerting his company.

Cameron had seen enough. He dialed Lang. It went to voicemail twice before she answered. "This has better be fucking good."

"I think Amy broke into my apartment sometime after she kidnapped Jaden and before we came home," he told her. "There is a very slim possibility Jaden is being held at my cabin in the

Muskokas."

"Hang on, how do you know that?"

"Did CSU ever figure out how she bypassed Jaden's security system?"

"They said it was a bypass loop into another person's system, why?"

"The same thing happened to my system here. I'm going to call building management, see if they can send today's tapes to you. I'm heading to my cabin. In the meantime, see if local PD can swing by and check it out. Wake everyone up."

"I'll handle it."

He returned to his bedroom and changed into black duty pants then dug into the back of his closet. He removed the thigh holster for his service weapon and his backup gun from his safe, as well as the second set of keys to his cabin he kept locked up just in case. He strapped on a bulletproof vest and pulled a black sweater on overtop, hiding the backup gun secured at the small of his back and his vest. He secured his service weapon to his thigh.

Paul had his jacket and boots on, and waited by the door when Cameron emerged.

"You're not coming with me."

He put on his black windbreaker, taking care to tuck in the reflective part that read POLICE.

"Yes, I am. I know you don't want to me to, but this involves me as much as it involves you. I won't get in the way."

Against his better judgment, he nodded. "Fine, let's go."

Outside, three cruisers waited.

The female patrol officer approached him. "I'm Sergeant Davis. I've been assigned to drive you. We'll take Detective Black's SUV."

"Sure."

Cameron handed over the keys and climbed into the passenger seat. Paul took the rear.

She started the lights and sirens and took off, the three other cruisers running interference for them. Despite being the middle of the night, the streets of Toronto were still busy, and anything that got him there faster gave him hope.

His cell phone rang. "Olsen," he snapped, over the roar of the siren.

"It's Lang. We got a positive ID on the perp entering your apartment about forty minutes after Jaden was kidnapped. She left three minutes later. I talked with local PD; they're going to send an officer to the cabin as soon as they can spare one."

"What do you mean as soon as they can spare one?"

Jaden was probably lying in his cabin, hurt—could even be dead—and they couldn't spare an officer to go see if anyone was even there?

"You don't have any proof Jaden is there, and it looks like they had a homicide about an hour away from the cabin. A domestic murder-suicide. All of the available officers in the area are tied up with that."

Cameron indulged in a stream of loud and vicious curses. He had a sinking feeling the murder-suicide was just a distraction for the local police. It confirmed, in his own mind anyway, he would find Jaden at the cabin. The question of how Amy knew about the rustic getaway still bugged him, though.

"Get them there as soon as you can. I'll leave the main gate unlocked once I arrive. Cell phone service is spotty there, so you might not be able to reach me. Davis has her radio on channel three. Advise the local PD that will be the best way to reach us. I'll also e-mail you directions to the cabin from the gate. The road can be confusing if you don't know where you're going."

"I'll do my best to get them there as soon as possible." She disconnected.

Leaving the city, they still had the occasional unit run interference for them, but for the most part, they were on their own. Davis had her foot to the floor, and they topped speeds of well over 220 kilometers per hour. The distance flew by, and, less than an hour later, she pulled off the main highway onto a country road.

Cameron called Lang again before they were out of cell range. The provincial police had promised they would be there in less than an hour. At the speeds Davis drove, they were ten minutes away from the main road to his cabin.

He directed her—right, left, and another right onto a gravel road. Straight down the road for another two kilometers before she took a final left. The wheels of the SUV slid on the loose dirt, and she fishtailed around the corner.

She pulled to a stop at the barred road, and he jumped out of the SUV. Running to the gate, he unlocked it, swinging it open. Davis pulled through the entrance, and he clambered back into the passenger seat.

"Kill the lights," Cameron ordered.

She did and stopped the flashing red and blue, along with the running lights. He guided her by the dim moon and stars, instructing her to take the higher road leading to the cabins above his own so no one would be alerted to their presence. She pulled in front of a cottage on the upper road and killed the engine.

He turned to Paul. "Stay here. Davis and I will head down and check it out. She'll come for you when we know it's safe."

Paul, who had been silent the entire drive to the cabin, just nodded in response.

They left the safety of the SUV and crept forward. By memory, Cameron walked the path from his neighbor's house, using the light from the low-hanging moon. Davis followed behind him. They approached the cabin from the hillside above and circled around to the path leading to it from the right side. Being early fall, the forest floor lacked the usual layer of dried leaves that could give away their position, and they glided down the slope moving from mossy patch to mossy patch.

As he got closer, he could smell wood smoke—there were flickers of light from the front of the cabin—as if a fire had been lit in the hearth of his master bedroom. He crept closer to the deck. At maybe a hundred feet away and on the hill, slightly above, he had the perfect view of the windows.

The figure of a woman walked around his bedroom—just one. *Amy.* If his dream was right, Jaden would be hidden in the crawlspace under the utility room.

"Our perp is the one in the front room there," he told Davis in hushed tones.

She nodded.

"That's the master bedroom. There are three doors to the cabin. The master bedroom has a set of french doors. There is the main door on the other side of the cabin, and a third door that leads into one of the small bedrooms."

"One of us distracts her to the front door and the other goes in the second door?" Davis crouched low next to him. Her shoulders hunched, her knees coiled tight, her training taking over as they faced danger—alone.

"I want you to draw her to the front of the cabin, then try and gain entry through the side door. If you can't, pull out, and wait for backup."

"How are you going in?"

"Got a pen?"

Davis reached into her vest and produced the implement.

He took it from her.

"The french doors are only supposed to unlock from the inside, but I've locked myself out enough times to know a pen will open them from the outside. Hopefully, that will allow me to surprise her when she comes back into the master bedroom."

"Are you sure you don't want to wait for backup?" Davis asked.

"I'm sure. If you don't want to do this, I'll go in alone."

Davis shook her head, her short ponytail bobbing. "Let's do this."

She moved away, making her way to the other side of the cabin.

Moving as close as he dared to the cabin, he watched the figure, waiting for her to move. He heard a loud crash at the front of the cabin, and the figure stepped away from the window.

Cameron took a deep breath. *Showtime.*

Chapter Twenty-One

*H*e bolted for the doors and then wiggled the pen in between them. It took him two tries before the lock clicked and the door opened. He slid inside and shut the door. He scanned the bedroom illuminated by the light from the fireplace. A haphazard pile of blankets had been tossed onto the bed. Other than that, it appeared identical to the way he had left it the last time he had visited. He went to the door and pressed himself against the wall, hoping to grab Amy when she opened the door.

His ears strained to hear any sounds, but the silence seemed to press in around him. He listened for footsteps, or the door opening.... Nothing.

He held his breath, not daring to breathe in case it gave him away. The crackle of Davis's radio broke the silence. *Shit.*

He drew his weapon. Pointing it at the floor, he eased the door open and glanced around the corner to check that the coast was clear. A scuffle came from the second small bedroom, and he advanced through the hallway toward the door.

The double tap gunshot seemed to reverberate from the cabin, no doubt wakening the woods around it and echoing off of the lake. His adrenaline started pumping twice as fast as before. He cleared the first small bedroom then made his way to the second one. Pressing himself against the wall, he opened the door with his left hand. It swung inward, and he used the mirror in his pocket to glance around the frame. Davis lay on the floor, and Amy stood over her, holding a gun.

"Drop the weapon, Amy," he ordered. His voice boomed through the cabin. "Drop the weapon and put your hands in the air."

Amy spun around and grabbed Davis by the vest, jerking her to her feet. She pressed the gun to the officer's temple. "Come on out, Detective Olsen, or the next bullet she takes will be in her head not her vest."

Shit. He hesitated, but he heard her cock the gun.

"Show yourself, Olsen," she screamed. "Three, Two—"

Cameron stepped into the doorway.

"Drop the gun," she ordered.

"I can't do that, Amy."

He deliberately kept his gun pointed downward as he took a step toward her.

"Don't come any closer, or I'll blow her head off." She jabbed the muzzle of the gun into Davis' head.

"All right, I'm not going any closer. Why don't you let Sergeant Davis go?"

"Drop your gun," she demanded. "Now."

Cameron paused, considering his options. He then unloaded the magazine with the briefest flick of his wrist, slipping it into his sleeve. He didn't keep a round in the chamber, so he dropped the unloaded gun to the floor. "There you go. The gun is on the floor. I'm unarmed."

"Kick it toward me."

Davis' radio crackled again, asking for a status update, which meant backup had to be close—he just had to keep her talking.

He kicked the gun toward her.

"Let Sergeant Davis go."

Amy smiled and pistol-whipped Davis before tossing her to the floor. She moaned but remained motionless. He wasn't sure if she'd been knocked out or was just pretending, but he went with the assumption his colleague was unconscious for the moment and unable to help.

"Where's Paul?" Her gun trained on him, she bent and picked up his gun, tucking it into the back of her pants.

"In Toronto," he lied.

"He wouldn't stay in Toronto, not if he thought Jaden was here. He always cared more about precious Jaden than anyone else."

"He's at my condo in Toronto. I wouldn't let him come with me. It was too dangerous."

"Then why is he outside?" Amy moved to the door and opened it, her gun still trained on Cameron. "Get in here, Paul."

Paul stepped out of the shadows and into the doorway. Amy took a step forward and grabbed Paul by the arm, shoving him forward into the cabin, then she closed and locked the door.

"I told you to stay in the car."

"I heard the gunshots. I'm sorry."

"Shut up," Amy ordered. "Both of you. No talking."

"How did you know Paul was outside?" Cameron wanted to keep her as distracted as possible. Muffled tones came from Davis's radio—they were talking about something. He hoped it was backup getting closer.

Even in the darkness, Cameron could see her smirk. "I saw the movement out of the corner of my eye. Who else could it be? I know all of the local police are busy with that poor tragic triple murder-suicide. Shame he killed the kids as well as his wife, but you know, he always was a little unstable, especially when he was drinking."

Paul seemed stunned at her admission. "So, you killed an entire family for a distraction? Do you know what you're doing?"

"Of course I know what I'm doing. This isn't my first rodeo, Paul, not by a long shot."

Her Irish accent leaked into the posh and polished American one she had been using. Good, he was getting to her.

"Why are you doing this, Amy?" At least Paul was keeping her busy while Cameron strategized.

Davis's hand twitched ever so slightly. Like she just opened her emergency button on her mike, broadcasting everything that was happening in the cabin to the police, who were hopefully closing in on the location.

"Because I want what's rightfully mine."

"Amy, what are you talking about? What's rightfully yours?" Paul asked.

She laughed, shaking her head. "You always were clueless, Paul. I want to be telepathic, like I should have been born, like I should have been once I killed Adeline."

He gasped. "She died from a drug overdose."

"Yeah, she did, but I gave her the lethal dose. Poor misunderstood Adeline. It was easy once she passed out, drunk. I injected the heroin. Tragic really, since it was her first time trying the drug and she overdid it, but, hey, it was the eighties, right? What I didn't know at the time was, since you and Adeline were twins, I would have to kill both of you to inherit your powers."

"So, you came up with an elaborate plot to murder women that looked like Jaden. To do what? Scare her? Put her on alert?" Cameron asked.

Davis moved, her hand inched toward her service gun. He needed to keep Amy distracted until Davis got a chance to make her move.

"Make killing her that much more sweet?" he taunted. "Why the first three women without the notes?"

She shrugged. "I thought I would get Jaden's attention. I guess dumping them in the lake made them undesirable cases for her. I needed to get her attention."

"Why wait until now?" he asked, trying to keep her talking as long as possible.

"I needed the mating process to be complete, until I knew you slept with both of them. When that finally happened, I could kick my plan into gear. I've been waiting over two years for this moment."

The evil glint in her eyes scared him. He stood next to a genuine psychopath—no telling what she was capable of doing.

"Why?" he prompted again.

"Because the only way I could get her full power is to wait until you mated." She shook her head. "She might not even feel the difference yet, but it's there, growing inside her."

He shifted uncomfortably, not able to move properly until he got rid of the magazine hidden up his sleeve. "Why not just kill her in her sleep? Why the notes and the games?"

"I needed to get Paul here. They have to be killed almost at the same time for the powers to transfer together. I knew if I threatened Jaden, then he would come running. Paul's always had a soft spot for her, especially since I killed her parents."

"You started that house fire?" The anger in Paul's voice leaked through, and so did the fear. Amy had done everything she could to ruin both his life and Jaden's.

"Like I said, this is far from my first rodeo. I got away with it before, and I'll get away again. I might have burned this identity, but I have another much nicer one waiting for me."

A noise outside distracted Amy for a brief second.

Cameron slipped the magazine he held in his sleeve into his pocket. He could move better and not worry about tipping her off that the gun he'd tossed to her had been unloaded. "Who's out there?"

She glanced between her two hostages.

"The local police might be busy, but they know some of their own are in danger. They're going to come out in droves. You won't be able to escape, Amy. The best thing you can do is give yourself up." He kept his voice soft and took a step toward her.

"Stay back. They won't storm in here as long as they know I have you."

"I wouldn't be so sure." Trying to create some room for Davis to make a move, he took another step, forcing Amy to shift to the side.

"Back up. Both of you, into the bathroom. I want you to watch, Cameron, as I murder your precious mates. They say that when your mate is murdered, you feel like you've been killed as well. I wonder what it will feel like once both are dead?"

Cam frowned. "Why don't—?"

Amy leveled her gun at Davis. "Move or she's dead."

His stomached dropped. "All right, we'll go in the bathroom."

He glanced at Paul, giving him the smallest nod. Together, they took three steps backward. Amy followed, and Paul went into the hall first. Cameron had just stepped backward out of the room when shots were fired—three in quick succession.

Amy went down, and he jumped forward, kicking the gun from her grasp. He removed the other gun she had taken from him.

Davis lay on her back, her service weapon in her hands—she had fired three shots into Amy's center mass. As a result, blood gushed from her wounds. Cameron rolled her over.

She laughed. "I think that bitch shot me."

She giggled again. Bubbles of blood-filled air came from the corner of her mouth. One shot was a through wound, but the others must have hit her lungs.

He tried to stem the flow of blood. She wasn't going to die—dying was too good for her. The families of the people she had killed deserved justice. She needed to face her crimes.

The door exploded open, and two armed officers entered the tiny bedroom. Since Davis wore a uniform they turned to her first.

"Suspect is down. We need EMS," she said. One of them called it in. Davis holstered her weapon and crawled the few steps to where Amy lay sprawled in a growing pool of blood. "Go find Jaden. I'll stay here."

Nodding, Cameron rushed across the hall and into the bathroom, finding Paul already trying to force the door.

"It's locked." He rammed his shoulder into the door.

Cameron cursed—he didn't have a key for the old door.

"Stand back." Cameron leveraged himself against the counter and kicked twice before the jam splintered open. He pulled the door away and grabbed the string hanging from the light bulb. Almost blinded by the sudden light, he dropped to his knees, grabbing at the handle in the floor. He pulled on the trap door, flinging it open. Underneath the floorboards, Jaden moaned, and he jumped down into the crawlspace.

"Jaden, can you hear me?" Cameron shook her gently "Jaden?" She moaned. "Hey, we need some help in here." He yelled to Paul.

He bent down and picked Jaden up. Like a ragdoll, she flopped against him. With Paul's help, he lifted her onto the utility room floor. She moaned again. She had a large scrape on her forehead, and her face was swollen like she had been beaten, but she was alive. He climbed out of the crawlspace, snapped the trapdoor shut then gathered Jaden into his arms.

One of the local officers walked in. "I've called for EMS. How is she doing?"

"Alive." Cameron turned his attention to Jaden. "Darling, come on, wake up. Give me something."

She stared at him, her eyes focusing. She raised her hand and made some sort of sign.

"She says she's okay," Paul translated. Then Paul made some signs, and she replied. "Whatever Adeline gave her is blocking her telepathic abilities. She can't hear you."

"Can't hear me?"

Paul gave him the most exasperated look he'd ever seen. "Jaden's deaf."

He didn't get a chance to fully process that statement. EMS arrived and started accessing Jaden. He answered their questions as best he could, but they loaded her onto the stretcher and took her away. Cameron followed, but when they would only let one-person ride with her, he sent Paul. His heart broke as the ambulance drove off. He had to believe she would be okay with her protector looking after her until he could get there.

He went inside the cabin again. Davis sat on the couches in the great room, having yet another set of EMS personnel attend to her. A man with sergeant's stripes barked orders at other police officers, and various personnel wandered around the place.

Cameron sat next to Davis. "How are you doing?"

"Okay." Her hand trembled as she ran her fingers over her

empty holster—her gun had been taken as evidence. "They're not sure if she'll make it or not." Her lip quivered. "I shot her in the back. I shot someone in the back."

"I know it must have been hard, but you did the right thing," he assured her. "Your actions saved all of our lives tonight."

She nodded. "Thank you."

"I'm sorry I put you in that situation. I should have waited for backup."

"Damn right you should have," the sergeant barked at him from across the main room of the cabin. "Do you have any idea what situation you put us in, Olsen? That was an incredibly stupid decision."

"I'm sorry, sir," he apologized. "You're totally right, my actions were out of line, and I could have gotten a lot of people killed tonight." He would do it again in a heartbeat to save his partner.

The sergeant stared hard at him before he relaxed. "It might have been stupid, but I can't say I would have done something different in your situation. A couple of detectives are on their way. Once they're done interviewing all of you"—his gaze darted between the two of them—"then you'll be free to go."

"Thank you, sir," he replied.

It didn't take long for Lang to arrive. They interviewed Davis first while waiting for a third ambulance to make it to the cabin before taking her to the hospital to assess her for damage done by the bullets she took to the vest.

He waited for them to finish with Davis before he recounted the entire night's events to Lang and a detective from the Provincial Police. He repeated his story three times, when they were satisfied with his answers, they released him. A report from the hospital came in just as he was leaving—Amy died in the air ambulance en route to Toronto. He closed his eyes and sent out a silent prayer for Davis and her mental health at taking another person's life.

The sergeant also informed him Jaden was being admitted to the small local hospital in stable condition, and offered to drive him over there. He declined and headed out into the fresh September air. He climbed the path to where they'd left the SUV, leaving behind the cabin, the horrors it held, and the flashing emergency lights. The peace of the woods surrounded him as he walked. Once he reached the car, he unlocked it and slid into the driver's seat. Resting his head on the wheel, he let all of the emotions he had been holding in go, and cried.

Chapter Twenty-Two

Cameron pulled the SUV into his condo parking lot. Jaden snored ever so slightly, fast asleep in the back, with a pillow and a blanket. The hour and a half drive from the hospital had exhausted her. He climbed out and opened her door.

"Jay," he said, giving her a gentle shake. "*Jay.*"

"*Yeah. Sorry, did I fall asleep?*"

"*It's okay. Come on.*" He unbuckled her seatbelt and lifted her.

Jaden made a noise in her throat. She didn't squirm, but a strong fist pounded into his chest to tell him her displeasure at being carried inside. He didn't care. She was still weak and sore from her ordeal with Amy. The three days Jay had spent in the hospital felt like a lifetime to him.

For the first time in their relationship, everything lay open and bare. She'd told it all to him, her story, her secrets, her world, and he'd told his to her. Everything from their hopes and dreams to their history, and even why she'd hid her deafness from him for so long.

Paul met them at the main entrance to the building and opened the door for them, then followed them upstairs before opening the door to his condo for him. Cam set her on her feet in the hallway, standing next to her in case she fell. She didn't falter as she walked inside, and a cheer went up from the assembled group.

Jaden turned to Cameron. *"Jerk!"*

She landed another punch to his chest. Thankfully, she didn't hit very hard.

The small welcome home party had been Ruth's idea. She wanted to make sure Jaden knew she was loved and how grateful everyone was she was home and safe.

Jaden turned to the gathered group. *"Thank you,"* she thought, loudly enough so everyone could hear her.

The people in the room engulfed her with hugs. Cameron hung out in the kitchen, getting food ready and watching as Jaden stopped to speak with everyone, thanking them for their support.

Davis broke away from the gathering first, joining him in the kitchen. Bruises lined her skin just beneath her shirt collar. She'd taken two bullets in the vest at near point-blank range, and while the vest had saved her life, she was still battered from the impact.

"How are you feeling?" he asked her.

"Sore, but okay. I heard from IA today. They called it a good shoot. I still have some mandatory medical leave, then some counseling and desk duty, but should be back out there in two, maybe three months."

"I'm sorry."

"Not your fault. It's part of the job. I knew the risk when I volunteered to take you there, and I knew the risk going in without backup. I'm just grateful we made it out unscathed for the most part."

"I'm still sorry."

"It's still okay."

She helped Cameron put some cheese and snacks on a plate before bringing it into the living room. Chris joined him in the kitchen next, carrying a small boy with curly blond hair and blue eyes.

"Hi," he chirped at Cameron.

"Hi there. You must be Noel."

The boy nodded proudly.

"I hope it's okay I brought him," Chris said. "His foster mom asked me to take him today."

Cameron smiled. "It's fine. Are you having fun, buddy?"

"It's fun to meet real police officers."

"Hey, what am I? A fake police officer?" Chris tickled him, and Noel giggled. "I was wondering if we could get some juice for this little guy?"

"Sure, I think we have apple and some orange." He opened the fridge. Chris handed him a sippy cup he had been carrying. "Half-apple, half-water if you wouldn't mind."

Cameron poured the requested amounts into the cup and screwed the top on. He handed it to Noel.

"Thank you." He took the cup.

"Hey, buddy, why don't you go see Uncle Logan in the living room, okay?" Chris set Noel on the floor. "I'll be there in a minute."

Noel ran into the living room.

"He seems great," Cameron said.

"He is." Chris smiled. "I wanted to tell you we brought Jaden's laptop. Logan took off all phishing software, which looked like the main source of the leak. The perp accessed her files and shared whatever she had on the case to the media. Also the perp got onto your home computer—which explains how she knew about your cabin."

"What do you mean, main source?"

He digested the fact Amy had brought Jaden to his cabin because she had been peering into his computer using the Internet. That gave him the creeps.

"There is still some information leaked to the media doesn't seem like Amy could have released. That isn't general knowledge, FYI."

Cameron nodded—he understood the warning. Someone out there didn't have Jaden's best interests at heart. "Thanks for letting me know."

"No problem. How's she doing?"

"Okay, I think. She hasn't said much about what happened. She's been a lot quieter than usual. How's the Meincke investigation going anyway?"

"Nice change of subject—and it's being wrapped up. Since Meincke was a member of the provincial Police and from Toronto PD, they're bringing in an independent police investigator from Prince Edward Island, of all places, to review all our actions. The final charges against Meincke will be twelve counts of murder one, twelve counts of kidnapping, forcible confinement, and a dozen or more other charges—I can't remember."

Cameron let out a low whistle. "Have they identified all the girls yet?"

Chris shook his head. "Some of them date to his days as an investigator in Ottawa. We're still looking into his other, current, and past properties. He spent time in the military, so he moved around a lot. God knows how many other charges he's going to face."

"I can't believe he's gotten away with this for so long." Chris glanced into the living room. Noel sat on Logan's lap, chatting to Ruth non-stop, who appeared enamored with the small boy.

"Neither can I. He's a master manipulator, but he's been devolving. When perps devolve they start making mistakes. He just made enough that we caught him, and he'll be going away for what will amount to the rest of his life."

"Good. Son of a bitch should rot in hell. Let us know if you need any help with the independent investigation. We're off for the foreseeable future, but we'll be going stir-crazy after a little while."

"I'll let you know if I need anything." Chris sighed. "I can't help but feel the fact Jaden got kidnapped was somehow our fault. I mean if we hadn't asked you to meet us there, Amy never would have gotten to her."

"She knew where I lived, Chris, she knew everything about us. No matter what, she would have gotten to Jaden. I'm just thankful no one else was hurt." Cameron tamped down the guilt welling in his chest. He glanced into the living room and caught a glimpse of Jaden laughing with Paul. He had no idea what he would do if he lost her. He was just starting to find her.

Noel ran into the kitchen and attached himself to Chris, effectively ending their adult conversation. The party petered out half an hour later. Ruth came over to give them hugs when Nate stopped in. He returned to his first half-day of patrol after being assigned to Jaden. Cameron liked the young officer. He had the courage, determination, and dependability to go far in the force. Cameron knew he felt guilty about Jaden, but Nate hadn't been the one who said Jaden was fine to go to the bathroom on her own. If anyone should feel guilty, he should, but Jaden didn't blame anyone but Amy.

Once everyone had left, Jaden went to lie down in his bedroom. The trip home and the party had exhausted her. Paul helped him wash the dishes in the kitchen.

"I'm glad to have her home," Paul said, after a long but comfortable silence.

"I am, too." He dried his hands on a kitchen towel. "I thought I'd lost her."

His lover closed the short distance between them. He pulled Cameron into a tight embrace. They held each other close, kissing.

"I thought I'd lost both of you. It made me realize how much I love you. Both of you." Paul choked up a little.

He felt the same way, his throat thick with emotion. "I love you, too. I know it's crazy, and we have so much to learn about each other, but I love you."

They held each other, oblivious to everything else, until he felt a soft touch on his arm.

"*Hey.*" Jaden stared at them. "*Room in that hug for me?*"

Cameron partially released Paul and snuggled Jaden close to him. She smelled like she always did, felt like she always did, but somehow, they were different.

"*I feel it, too,*" Jaden whispered only to him. "*We're different. We've lived through something so terrible, and we've survived. We'll never be the same.*"

"*I still love you. I love you more than anything, Jaden. It's taken the past week to see it, but I've always loved you.*"

"*I love you, too,*" she replied.

Cameron let Paul go to gather his partner into his arms. He kissed her, his tongue exploring every facet of her mouth before she pulled away.

She turned to Paul and had a similar mental conversation with him. Paul kissed her cheek before turning to him. Their mouths met, powerfully claiming each other as their own. They were falling in love, and however it happened, it worked for them.

As they kissed, his vision went blurry, and he saw a brief glimpse of three dragons—one green, one black, and one red—all lying on top of a mound of treasure, deep in a cave, safe from the outside world.

"I'm thinking of staying," Paul announced once they broke apart, Cam's vision disappearing. "I love Australia, but I think I've found my place here."

"*What about the rescue?*"

Paul brushed the hair off of her face. "I've only been doing that for fun, luv. I've been semi-retired for years. I can move back here. Be a househusband. While you're out fighting crime, I can be doing the washing-up."

Jaden giggled at Paul's idea, but she hugged him close. "*I would love for you to move here, but I don't want to stay in my condo, though.*" A dark shadow passed over her face. "*I don't feel safe there anymore.*"

"I don't blame you," Paul replied. "I could always sell it, use the money to buy a nice house for us in the suburbs."

"For us?" Cameron asked.

"For all of us. I have no idea how it's going to work, but I'd like for us to give it a go."

"I would, too," he admitted.

"*Me three,*" Jaden said. "*I think we were meant to be together, and we'll take each day as it comes—however it comes.*"

"I like that," Paul said.

"I do as well."

Cameron pulled Paul toward him, kissing him before letting him go and kissing Jaden. Whatever else happened, today, tomorrow, or next week, he was happy and content in this moment. His lover, his partner—his mates—were safe in his arms, and that was all that mattered.

About the Author

Angela, is a twenty something Registered Nurse living in Ottawa, Canada. Angela finds inspiration in real life personal events for her books, often writing about issues she's experience in her life. She is a proud Canadian and an even prouder girl from back east. She thoroughly enjoys writing novels featuring character that live in or are from the Maritimes. She's recently met Mr. Right and when she's not occupied with him she can be found hanging out at her local Bridgehead writing. She spends her free time advocating for minorities and persons with disabilities.

www.angelastone.ca

74102784R00122

Made in the USA
Columbia, SC
28 July 2017